PROTECTING THE Princess

A ROYAL SECRETS ROMANCE

PROTECTING THE Princess

A ROYAL SECRETS ROMANCE

LUCINDA WHITNEY

Lange House Press

To Rosarita, from Mamacita.
This one's for you, even if you don't read it.

Chapter One

*E*mma Somerset stopped in front of the queen's office and took a deep breath. She slid her palms down the side of her black trousers and waited a few beats to calm her breathing. Then she rapped on the door.

Mr. Poe, the queen's secretary, opened it for her with a quiet "Your Highness."

As usual, he didn't comment on her lack of punctuality as he left the room, but Emma winced in silent apology as she passed him. She was ten minutes late, and the queen's distaste for tardiness was legendary.

"Emma, dear. There you are," said Queen Nicolette.

She greeted Emma with two kisses on each cheek in the true fashion of her home country of Galia, a habit she'd never lost with her family and closest friends.

"I'm sorry I'm late, Aunt Nicolette."

A man in a dark-gray suit stood to the side of her aunt's desk and Emma glanced at him. Who was he? She couldn't remember meeting him recently or seeing his picture before. Something about his straight posture and neutral presence gave her the impression this was a man who didn't like to stand out, which was oddly in opposition to his physical appearance and height. With his understated elegance and dark-haired good looks, he wouldn't be easily ignored.

He returned Emma's gaze with a carefully cultivated blank expression, and her interest stirred—he intrigued her, and she couldn't remember the last time a man had.

"Am I interrupting something?" Emma asked her aunt. "I can return later if that's more convenient."

"No, no," Aunt Nicolette replied quickly. She took Emma by the elbow and guided her forward. "I called you here to meet Mr. Ryan Sterling." She turned to the man. "Mr. Sterling, this is my niece, Princess Emma Somerset."

He tipped his head toward Emma in a brief bow. "Your Highness."

"Mr. Sterling." Emma nodded back at him.

Aunt Nicolette took her favorite upholstered chair, and Emma sat on the nearby sofa. Mr. Sterling remained standing until Aunt sent a quick nod his way, after which he took a straight-backed chair. He was acting more like an employee than a guest. What was he here for?

"I heard back about Ms. Allen's condition," Aunt Nicolette said. "She needs surgery and physical therapy, which means she'll be on medical leave for quite some time. After talking to Mr. Peters, we decided some changes were necessary for maintaining your protection."

Emma's stomach dropped. Mr. Peters was the head of security, in charge of all other security and personal protection officers who served the royal family. Lisa Allen, her personal bodyguard, had suffered an ankle fracture last night when she'd been jogging as she did everyday. Emma had been told someone would replace her soon.

She hadn't expected a guy in his early thirties with broad shoulders and a brooding gaze.

Emma gestured with her palm toward Mr. Sterling. "Him? He's my new PPO?"

"Emma," Aunt Nicolette chided.

"I apologize," Emma replied in an appropriately subdued tone. "I didn't mean to be disrespectful." She looked at Mr. Sterling, who remained impassive and unperturbed in his seat. He gave new meaning to the strong, silent type, what with the way he schooled his features to keep his thoughts hidden. Her new personal protection officer.

Aunt Nicolette continued. "Mr. Sterling came highly recommended by Mr. Peters, who assured your uncle and I that Mr. Sterling is the best for your current needs. Besides, on such short notice, we couldn't find a female protection officer. I know you and Charlotte always had female officers when you were growing up, but you're older now."

Emma nodded. It was true. Her twenty-sixth birthday was in a few months, but that didn't mean she needed a man tailing her every move.

How had Uncle Geoffrey and Aunt Nicolette gone along with this plan? This was not going to work. Lisa had been Emma's bodyguard for years and years; they knew each other's dynamic and their working relationship meshed well with each other's personalities. It was bad enough that Lisa was out of commission for some weeks, or even months, but a male bodyguard working as her replacement, however temporarily, was not a good idea. How was she going to carry out her little plan with a new guy following her around?

Emma took a breath and held silent for a moment, keeping a placid expression while her mind tried to work out a solution. Arguing with Aunt Nicolette would lead nowhere; Emma and Charlotte and the boys had learned that the hard way in their younger years. Aunt Nicolette seldom changed her mind unless there was a valid reason to persuade her.

"Mr. Sterling will take his position immediately," Aunt added. "You'll need to hand him your schedule and list of duties so he becomes familiar with your activities and responsibilities in time for your upcoming trip."

Aunt Nicolette stood and reached for her tablet on her desk, and Mr. Sterling immediately rose from his chair, standing beside it. Emma kept her gaze away from him, trying to disguise her conflicted interest and how his forced presence was going to disrupt her life. It was almost too much at once, after months and months of nothing out of the ordinary.

"Mr. Poe has finalized your itinerary to Edenshire, Meeds, and Inverly and sent a copy to your inbox." She tapped on the screen. "The date was changed, by the way."

Hope surged for a second. "For later?"

"I'm afraid not. For early next week." Aunt Nicolette rattled off the dates for each location.

Emma pulled out her phone to look over her schedule and sighed audibly. There was a property in Hillside Meadows she wanted to visit on one of those days. Would she be able to postpone the appointment with the land agent? And how would she get there, now that Lisa wasn't her PPO? Emma couldn't very well request a car and driver for an errand two hours away from the palace; someone would want a reason and an explanation. Someone always did.

"Must I be the one to go, Aunt?"

"We've been over this, Emma. I need your help, and I think you're the perfect person for this trip."

She was the only person who could go—Charlotte was in South Africa, and all the boys were married and had various duties that took precedence. As the last single child in the Somerset family, without the responsibilities that came from being attached to a significant other, Emma was the obvious choice to go on a good-will trip to visit children's hospitals in the northwestern region of the country.

"Yes, of course, Aunt."

She'd keep her opinions to herself, even if it hurt her to do so. As much as she preferred to not go on this trip, Emma was incapable of saying no to Aunt Nicolette, both for personal reasons and out of a sense of duty. After all, Aunt Nicolette and Uncle Geoffrey had certainly done their obligation and more, stepping in to care for Oliver and Emma eighteen years ago after their parents died in an accident.

"Thank you, dear," Aunt said as she rounded her desk and sat back down. "When you return, ask Mr.

Poe to put a lunch with you on my schedule so we can discuss ideas for your charity project."

Emma left her chair, and her smile came unbidden. "I'd love that, Aunt Nicolette. Thank you."

Her plans for a charitable foundation to benefit children were not coming as easily as the ideas she'd first had. Input from Aunt Nicolette would be more than welcome, and a lunch date sounded perfect. As busy as Aunt was with her many royal duties, Emma appreciated the offer. If only Aunt were as open to discussing Emma's trust fund situation, maybe Emma could make some progress with her plans to move out of the palace. She wouldn't put it past her aunt to send her on this trip as a way to get a break from Emma's constant requests for more independence.

"It's settled, then. Now, why don't you and Mr. Sterling meet in the small library to discuss the itinerary and your schedule? I'm sure you both have logistics to talk about."

Mr. Poe reentered the office and approached the desk, standing next to it. How did he do that? Always arriving at the perfect moment. That was Emma's cue to leave.

"Thank you for coming, Mr. Sterling," Aunt Nicolette said, already giving her attention to a folder Mr. Poe had brought.

"Yes, ma'am," Mr. Sterling said.

He held the door open, and Emma led the way across the hall. "Right this way."

Somehow, he managed to arrive before her in time to open the next door for her. Although she was used to that kind of deference, especially when in the palace, his attention felt personal. But it wasn't, and she'd do well to remember that.

The small library wasn't small by normal standards—only when compared to the official library on the main floor of the palace. This one was located closer to the family's personal wing and was also used by secretaries and assistants as the need arose.

The room was long and narrow, anchored by floor-to-ceiling bookshelves filled with volumes that covered many topics and categories. Opposite the door, a wide desk from the eighteenth century stood in front of two large windows, and an ornate marble fireplace acted as the focal piece, flanked by a classic a leather sofa and matching chairs. Tucked in the left corner by the door, a wooden hutch and desk housed the modern conveniences of phone, printer, and charging stations for wireless devices.

Emma lowered herself onto one of the leather chairs. "Let's have a seat, Ryan." She indicated a chair opposite hers. "May I call you Ryan?"

"Yes, of course, ma'am."

He managed to sit down and still keep his posture at attention, as if waiting for an imminent threat. Did he ever relax?

For a moment, they watched each other. Emma didn't know what to make of this man, who was now responsible for her protection and who'd be following her closely in public.

"I have to be honest," she started. "I wasn't expecting a male protection officer."

"Is it going to be a problem, ma'am?"

She resisted the temptation to roll her eyes at him. "Are you always like this?"

His eyes took on an earnest expression. "Like what, Your Highness?"

"So fervent about following protocol and using titles every time you address me. I'm not the queen of Durham, you know."

"Yes, I am quite aware, ma'am."

Was that a trace of humor behind his professional demeanor? She didn't know him enough to tell. Hopefully he had a lighter side to his personality or their daily interactions would be staid and boring. Emma abhorred boredom.

"Coming back to your question, you being a male is less of a problem and more of a surprise." Unless he made it a problem. "Lisa Allen has been my protection officer since my brother and I moved in with Uncle Geoffrey and Aunt Nicolette."

"That's a long time."

"It is." In truth, Emma had gotten used to having Lisa in her day-to-day life. "After Lisa got hurt last night, Mr. Peters called and assured me I'd have a new protection officer today. And here you are." Maybe she should have asked Mr. Peters more questions before assuming he'd send a female officer.

"I expect there will be a period of adjustment for both of us," Ryan Sterling said.

"Right. That's a good point. Adjustments are necessary. Which leads into what I wish to bring up with you. Before anything else, we need to establish some simple rules to make the transition smoother."

He frowned for a second but quickly resumed his expression of neutrality. If she hadn't been watching him, she would have missed it.

"I understand the need to observe protocol when we're in public, but at other times, you don't need to use *Your Highness* or *ma'am* to address me."

He paused for a beat, then replied, "Very well, Princess Emma."

Was he being facetious? "When we're in private, like we are right now, you may call me just Emma."

His left eyebrow pulled up, but he didn't comment.

Emma continued. "When I'm in the palace, I won't require your presence, obviously. I will need you mostly for public outings and official visits. Private outings are excluded as well."

"Private outings?" he questioned. "To clarify, what is a private outing, ma'am?"

Now she'd said too much.

Chapter Two

*A*t Ryan's question, Princess Emma looked away, but he still caught her eye roll.

Did she mean she went out by herself?

She was proving to be more difficult than he'd anticipated.

When Ryan had applied to be a personal protection officer for the royal family, he never thought he'd be babysitting the youngest princess of Durham. Was she going to be like this all the time?

He'd worked as a personal protection officer for a business mogul with international assets and interests for several years, but the traveling got tiring after a while, and he'd been ready for a change and a new position. He thrived on new challenges, but this was one he hadn't foreseen.

Princess Emma cleared her throat and glanced away before looking back at him. Her eyes were bluer than he'd expected, almost unsettling, and he hoped to get used to them—to her—soon enough. He didn't like feeling unsettled.

"Well, a private outing is when I need to be by myself," she added. "Nothing special."

Just as he'd guessed—she went out in public unaccompanied. He cringed inside at the thought of a member of the royal family, immediate family at that, going out lacking the protection of a personal officer. Was no one aware she did this? Where had her former protection officer been when Princess Emma went out?

He kept his expression impassive. "Do you do this often, Your Highness?"

She blinked slowly, probably irritated at his use of her title again. He wasn't doing it to vex her. Protocol was protocol, and he wouldn't break it because she didn't like it. Professionalism was important to him, and he prided himself on following procedure in all situations.

He'd been working at the palace for almost a month now, mostly training with the team of protection officers and learning the royal code of behavior while waiting to be assigned to a specific detail. In all honesty, Ryan had hoped to work for Prince Alexander and his family, but he lacked the experience for that position, and he knew that.

It hadn't even occurred to him that he'd be sent to Princess Emma, the youngest royal of the Somerset family. With Mr. Peters's recommendation to His and Her Majesties, Ryan hoped to gain both the experience and the trust in this new assignment that he would need for a higher-profile job. If he did it well, he'd get a chance at advancement with more responsibility. In the end, it would be worth it, and it would definitely look impressive on his résumé. It would only take some perseverance and time. And some patience, by the look of it.

As for the princess, she was more self-assured and confident than he'd expected, which he should have in the first place. She was born privileged and had grown up wanting for nothing; of course she'd be an assertive woman. He'd read the dossier his team leader had given him, but meeting the woman in person had made him aware of her strong personality. As long as she didn't turn out to be a spoiled brat; he didn't have any patience for that sort of behavior, especially in a grown woman.

She was also much more attractive in person than in the photos he'd seen of her, with her dark hair and blue eyes, a family feature she shared with some of her cousins. The effect on her was much more striking. But that had no bearing on his job, and he'd do well to forget her physical characteristics.

He focused his attention back on her as he waited for her reply.

"Not too often. It's not even worth mentioning." Her bright-blue eyes flashed at him, as if daring him to contradict her.

He wouldn't—not right now. If he wasn't mistaken, it sounded like she regretted telling him about her outings. Instead, he'd investigate, follow her if necessary, compile evidence, and then he'd go to Mr. Peters. Did she truly not understand the risk? If she did this on a regular basis, it had to stop. Not only was she endangering herself but also her family. Unbelievable.

"Very well, Your Highness. Let's discuss the upcoming trip, please," Ryan said. "What can you tell me about it?"

She visibly relaxed at the change of topic, which only reinforced his instincts.

"I'll be traveling to Edenshire, Meeds, and Inverly to visit children's wards and rural schools on my aunt's behalf."

Ryan removed his phone from his pocket. "Excuse me. I need to type some notes."

She waved her hand casually.

He opened the app and took some notes on his phone. He'd have to find out when the last royal visit to these towns had been. Most likely, he'd have to write up a new protocol for entering and exiting each place, but he'd check first with Princess Emma's former personal protection officer.

"Who else will be accompanying you?"

"A driver, probably Mr. Myles, and Mrs. Campion, one of the assistant secretaries. She will also be acting as the social affairs liaison."

He'd be requesting access to their files today. "Anybody else?"

She shook her head. "That's it."

That would not be it, if it was up to him. "A small entourage," he commented.

"Yes. It's one of the advantages in sending me on this trip, as I'm not as important and don't require as much attention."

He'd be the judge of that. "As far as I'm concerned, you're the most important."

Her eyes widened, and color stained her cheeks.

Belatedly, he realized how his words could be misunderstood. "You're my principal, the person I work for."

"I know what principal means," she replied quickly, her tone with a slight edge of irritation.

He felt the need to explain himself further. "It's my responsibility to watch over you first. That's why I said you're the most important to me."

"I know that's all you meant, Mr. Sterling. You don't need to clarify." She added a tight smile, almost bordering on a grimace.

He thought he'd been making some headway with her, but not now, as evidenced by the way she addressed him. Every new assignment came with a period of adjustment between him and his principal. Trust was an indispensable element, but it came slower in some relationships. In this case, he didn't have the time for a slow progression with Princess Emma, not with the trip so close. How was he supposed to build trust between them in such a short time?

She rose to her feet. "I have an appointment," she blurted. "You'll have to excuse me, but I need to go."

He slid his phone into his pocket as he stood from his chair, ready to accompany her out of the library.

She didn't wait for his reply, nor for him, already walking toward the hallway. "Let's continue this tomorrow. Do you have my phone number? What am I saying? Of course you have my number. You probably have all the numbers."

He followed right behind her. "Your Hi—"

"Shoe size, weight, height," she continued. "Who knows what other numbers you have."

Was she talking to him or to herself?

After a moment, she halted and turned around, holding her hand up. "Thank you, Mr. Sterling. That'll be all for today. Welcome to the team," she added.

"Thank you, Your Highness. It's my pleasure," he said to her retreating form, the echo of her heels lingering behind her on the parquet floor.

After she turned the corner at the end of the hallway, Ryan let out a deep breath.

It couldn't have gone worse, if he'd tried. The good news was, it would only get better from here. He hoped. It had to; his career goals depended on it.

"Mr. Sterling," a voice said. The queen's secretary appeared in the hallway. The man knew how to be stealthy.

"Yes, sir?"

"Her Majesty would like a word with you, please."

Ryan followed the secretary back inside Her Majesty's office, where she sat at her desk.

"How did it go with my niece, Mr. Sterling?" she asked.

What could he say that wasn't a lie or unfavorable to Princess Emma? "We discussed Her Highness's schedule, and we'll be meeting again tomorrow."

"You're a diplomat, I see," the queen replied, a gentle smirk at the corner of her mouth. "I know my niece, Mr. Sterling. She has a very independent spirit." She paused for a moment. "Emma has a kindness that comes naturally to her, but she's also impatient. I'd appreciate it if you could offer a gentle influence on her."

"You'd like me to influence Her Highness, ma'am?" Ryan was unable to keep the surprise from his tone. He'd barely met Princess Emma, but he could tell she wasn't the kind of woman who'd take influence where none was wanted.

"Think of it as a guidance of sorts. So she doesn't fall into trouble," the queen added.

"I'll do my best, ma'am." That was all he could promise.

After being dismissed, Ryan made his way to the security offices and requested the personnel files for the driver and the assistant secretary. Then he used one of the office computers to send an email to Princess Emma's former protection officer and to research the current travel protocols. He also emailed the head of security in each hospital of the towns she'd mentioned and sent his notes to himself to work on his laptop. Once back at his apartment, he'd be able to access his findings and put together a plan for the trip.

His team leader, Mr. Hankins, entered the room as Ryan logged out.

"Sterling, did you meet with Her Majesty and Princess Emma?"

"Yes, sir, I did."

"Good, good. Let me know if you need any help with Her Highness's trip."

"Thank you, sir. I'll keep that in mind."

Research and planning kept Ryan busy for the rest of the day, as he gathered everything he could find to prepare for the trip. Ideally, he would have had the time to scout the route, the hotels, and the hospitals, but that was simply not possible on such short notice. This time, he built his plan with previous protocols and notes from other protection officers. He would also need to meet with the assistant secretary to make sure she would add extra time for him to scan the premises at each location. Before he left, he got the names of two other agents and a second driver who were available to join the trip and made the requisitions for two additional vehicles. A small entourage didn't fit with his plans.

When he arrived at his apartment, Ryan was ready to call it a day and decompress. He slipped off his tie and hung up his suit jacket on a hanger behind the door, then rolled up his shirtsleeves as he looked around the small space.

There was nothing special about the one-bedroom and one-bathroom apartment with an open-concept kitchen and living room. It was less of a home and more of a place where he could return to at the end of the day to rest. What with working so many years abroad, he hadn't needed to own an apartment in Castlebridge, but now that he was back, maybe he would think about it.

His phone rang with the custom tone he'd assigned to his honorary grandmother. "Hi, Nana. How are you?"

"Ryan, dear. I'm so glad I caught you. It's been a while."

"It has, Nana. I'm sorry." He walked over to the sofa and sat down.

"It's all that traveling you do. Where are you right now?"

"I'm back in the country, Nana. I'm in Castlebridge."

"Castlebridge? That's only two hours away. When are you coming to visit?"

"I just started a new job, and I have a field assignment coming up."

"Who are you working for now?"

"I'm with the security team at the palace."

"That means you're working for the king and queen," she said excitedly.

"Indirectly, yes, I am."

"That's amazing. What an honor. They hire only the best, you know."

"They're supposed to. Not that I'm trying to brag," he added quickly.

"Of course not. You're too modest for that. When can I expect you?"

"As soon as I get a weekend off, I'll come see you, I promise."

"You make sure you do. I've missed you, Ryan."

"I've missed you too." She was right; it had been too long.

After hanging up with Nana, Ryan changed out of his suit pants and shirt and set up his laptop on the kitchen table to retrieve his notes from the research he'd done earlier in the day.

He checked his email and was relieved to find replies to his inquiries, as these would facilitate the first step of his research for the trip.

Tomorrow, when he met with Princess Emma, they'd discuss the specifics of the itinerary.

Ryan stopped in his thoughts. He had yet to arrange a follow-up meeting with Her Highness. It was too late to call, which meant a text would have to do, as if things between them weren't awkward enough already.

He pulled up her file on his laptop, found her number, and saved it into his contacts list on his phone.

Then he typed a brief message.

Your Highness, this is Ryan Sterling. Please let me know at what time you'd like to meet tomorrow, and where. Thank you.

He kept the phone on the tabletop with the screen facing up, but she didn't reply. Hopefully, she would in the morning.

The last thing he wanted to do was to impose the meeting on her, but they had to talk and make preparations. She might not think she needed him around, but he, at the least, planned to take her safety during the upcoming trip most seriously.

Chapter Three

Once in her apartment wing later in the evening, Emma called her best friend. "Charlotte, you won't believe what happened," she said when her cousin answered the video call.

"What happened? Is everyone all right? Was there any accident?"

At the sight of Charlotte's worried face, Emma hurried to explain. "Nothing bad. Sorry to alarm you. I was assigned a new PPO."

"Royal Security had Lisa replaced?"

"They did. She broke her ankle and will be on medical leave for some time."

"That's terrible. She's always been so active," Charlotte said. "But I guess she's not as young anymore."

"She can't be over fifty, can she?" Emma asked. She had no idea how old her former personal protection officer was. Lisa had never been forthcoming with the information, and Emma had never prodded.

"Who knows? She and Karla always appeared invincible to me." Karla had been Charlotte's protection officer.

"To all of us, I think."

"What's her name?" Charlotte asked.

"Whose name?"

"Your new PPO. How old is she?"

"My new PPO's name is Ryan Sterling."

On the phone's screen, Charlotte's eyes widened. "A man? Your new personal protection officer is a man?"

"You don't have to emphasize it, Char," Emma said, not caring to disguise her irritation. "And wipe that grin off your face."

"I'm not grinning. I'm shocked at this turn of events."

"You were definitely grinning. I called you to commiserate with me, and I'm not seeing any commiseration."

"I'm sorry, Em. I know you're upset, but you remember when we were fifteen and pled with Father to let us have male protection officers?"

Emma's lips stretched in a reluctant smile. "He told us it would never happen."

Charlotte smiled. "And now it has. After all this time. Tell me more about your Ryan Sterling," she added after a brief pause. "He has a great name."

"Does he? I didn't notice." She had noticed. "He insists on calling me *Your Highness* or *Princess Emma* or *ma'am* the whole time."

"Well, that's your title, and he has to use it. He probably doesn't want to be disrespectful."

"He follows protocol for everything. And he's not mine," Emma said, a bit too insistently.

"He is your PPO. What does he look like?"

Emma paused before replying. "He reminds me of James Kinnaird. The same kind of hooded eyes, tanned skin, and strong jaw."

The actor was one of Emma's and Charlotte's favorites and they had binge-watched several times the dystopian movie trilogy he starred in.

Charlotte chuckled lightly. "It sounds like he's handsome and you don't want to admit it."

"I'm not going to admit to anything because there's nothing to admit. I'm a little frustrated he's my new protection officer and I didn't get any input." She paused and sighed. "Maybe I'm overreacting."

"I'm sorry you're frustrated, Em. We grew up with Karla and Lisa and got so used to their presence, we never entertained the idea of having different bodyguards. And now that the boys are all married, and

I'm so far away, Mother and Father are focused on you."

"Argh, you're so right. It's the curse of the youngest. I need to move out."

"You need to get married," Charlotte said at the same time.

"Watch what you say, Char." Emma leaned over and tapped the closest coffee table three times with her knuckles. "I enjoy my single life, thank you very much. Besides, I have lots to do before I entertain the idea of matrimony. And you forget the most important part. I have to meet someone first."

"Maybe you've met him already and you don't know yet he's the one."

"That's just crazy, Charlotte."

"You never know. Crazier things have happened. Just look at me and Adam. You were right about us, so maybe I'm right about you."

"You don't have to look so smug about it. Now tell me, what am I going to do about this trip and my new PPO?"

"Who else is going?"

"Mrs. Campion and Mr. Myles."

Charlotte cringed. "Mrs. Campion needs to retire already. She's no fun. I'm surprised they still send her on trips."

Emma slumped and rested her chin on her hand. "I know. At least Mr. Myles isn't too bad, but who knows how any of this will turn out with Mr. Sterling coming along."

"You need to give him a chance, Em. You've just barely met him. He might prove better than your first assessment."

"Let's hope so." She sighed. "We have a meeting tomorrow morning, the two of us with Mrs. Campion and Mr. Myles. Mr. Sterling insisted on it."

"That proves he's thorough and likes to be prepared. Those are good qualities."

"He's only concerned about doing his job. To him, I'm just the principal he needs to protect."

"Aren't you being a little harsh? How do you know he feels that way?" Charlotte asked.

"Because he said so."

Charlotte frowned. "In those words?"

Emma nodded, then looked away from the screen, still embarrassed at the reaction she'd had earlier. "He asked why my entourage was so small for this trip, and I said it's because I'm not as important, to which he said I was the most important to him. And, Charlotte, I blushed. I felt my cheeks go hot, and my whole face must have turned red. He was very quick to explain I'm important to him because I'm his principal."

Charlotte stared for a moment. "You two are off to a great start, aren't you?"

Emma groaned. "It has to get better. We'll be spending a lot of time together, and I don't want it any more awkward than it already is. As if this wasn't enough, Aunt Nicolette moved up the trip, which means I won't be able to go see that one property in Hillside Meadows."

"Are Mom and Dad still not willing to call a lawyer to look into the trust clause?"

"They said it is the way it is and don't want to try to make any changes. How is it fair that the boys got their trusts at twenty-one and we have to wait until we're thirty?"

Charlotte winced. "Either age thirty or marriage, whichever comes first."

"Don't remind me. That's not fair either. This is the twenty-first century, after all. I shouldn't have to fight for my independence. How does having a husband make me more responsible?"

"Well—" Charlotte started.

"That was a rhetorical question, Char," Emma said, a bit too sternly. "Sorry. It's not you I'm mad at. I don't think it's too much to ask to be able to buy a house by myself and move out of the family unit." If she could call the palace that.

"I know. It's a reasonable request," Charlotte agreed.

Emma shook her head, as if that could release the doubt and uncertainty that had settled in her mind today. "Enough talk about me. Stand up and show me your little bump."

Charlotte grinned. She propped up the phone, stood, and walked away to grant Emma a full-body view. Then she turned sideways and cradled her belly. "My little bump is getting big."

"It looks adorable, and so do you."

"You think so? I feel so bloated all the time." She approached the phone and sat in front of it again.

"Definitely not bloated. Beautiful is more like it." Just last week, Charlotte had worn an outfit for a public function that had quickly made it into a maternity fashion blog. "How are you feeling overall?"

Charlotte's shoulders slumped. "Still pretty sick and useless, which brings me to the news I want to tell you. Adam and I finalized our plans last night, and you'll be the first one to know. Well, the second. I already told Mother."

"I have a hunch I'm going to love these plans."

Charlotte chuckled. "I'm positive you will." She paused for effect before continuing. "We're coming home for Christmas on December fourth."

Emma quickly pulled up the calendar app. "That's three whole weeks before Christmas. That's so great." She smiled wide and clapped.

"I know," Charlotte said in an excited tone. "Adam and I are hoping the renovations will go better when we're closer." Charlotte and Adam had bought an old manor house and were in the middle of renovations, planning to move shortly after the baby came. "I have a big favor to ask you," Charlotte continued.

"Anything you need."

"Mother said Adam and I can stay in my old apartment until the manor is finished, but the thought of overseeing another renovation, even one as small as this, makes me want to cry."

"I'll take over for you," Emma quickly offered. "I'm right here and I know everything you like, and you don't need to worry about it."

"You're the best, Emma," Charlotte said with visible relief. "You have no idea how much stress that takes off. Thank you so much."

"Of course. Don't even mention it. We should have thought of this before. Do you want to have any input?"

Charlotte winced. "Would you think any less of me if I said no? I just want to leave everything in your capable hands. Like you said, you know what I like."

"It'll be my pleasure, Charlotte. You focus on growing that little baby of yours and I'll do the rest here. Do you know the gender yet?"

"Adam and I decided to wait and be surprised."

"That will be fun."

"So maybe a neutral, classic nursery?"

"We can certainly do that," Emma assured, as ideas of an animal safari theme ran through her mind. Or should she go with a different theme instead?

"Are you sure you'll have the time? You'll be busy with that trip coming up."

"That's the only thing I have on my schedule. I have plenty of time to get your apartment ready for you and Adam and the baby. Do you have a return date planned?"

"Maybe in the late spring. Adam and I want the baby to be a little older before we make the trip back."

Emma smiled again. "Which means you'll have the baby christened here too."

Charlotte nodded with a smile of her own. "Definitely. We want our families present for it. I know we talked about this when we were younger, but the invitation to be the baby's godmother stands."

Emma brought a hand to her heart. "It was so long ago when we talked about being godmothers to each other's babies. I didn't want to presume."

"Do you accept then?"

"Of course. Thank you." She picked up a notebook to write down some ideas. At the corner of the screen, the high number of notifications caught her attention, and she swiped at it. One in particular stopped her. "He texted me." She stared at the name and the message for a moment.

"Who texted you?"

"Ryan Sterling. My notifications were off, and I didn't notice it until now."

"What did he say?"

Emma read the short message. "*Your Highness, this is Ryan Sterling. Please let me know at what time you'd like to meet tomorrow, and where.*"

"Didn't you say you already have a meeting scheduled?"

Emma forced herself to swipe away the text, unwilling to admit how much it had caught her by surprise. It shouldn't have.

"Are you all right?" Charlotte asked.

Emma relaxed her expression. "Yes, of course. The meeting is with Mrs. Campion and Mr. Myles. Mr. Sterling and I still need to talk about my schedule and activities." She'd rushed out when she'd met him this morning instead of staying longer to talk with him. That move had only postponed the problem, as they still had to talk in preparation for the trip.

"Are you not going to call him by his first name?"

"I was at first. We've always called Lisa and Karla by their first names. But something—" She paused and shook her head. "I don't know. It threw me off so much when I found out he's my new protection officer. I don't know what to do," she added after a pause.

"Maybe things will get better as you get to know each other," Charlotte said.

Was Ryan Sterling the sort of man who would let anyone to know him?

Chapter Four

"My scheduled has changed, Mr. Sterling," said Princess Emma to Ryan after the meeting in the morning.

After Mrs. Campion and Mr. Myles, and Officers Black and Little left the room, Princess Emma waited for him. He had noticed a different undercurrent about her, a thread of impatience, like she had held on to something and was only waiting to say it. So this was it, a change to her schedule.

"For next week, ma'am?"

"No, for this week. I took over a decorating project for my cousin Charlotte, and I need to get it set up before I leave on Monday."

"Very well, ma'am. If you'll give me a copy of your schedule, I'll start the planning."

"I'm afraid I'm not that kind of a planner." Her expression dropped for a moment. "I can only tell you what I'm doing today, and maybe tonight I call tell you what I'm doing tomorrow."

"I'm sure I can work with that," he said.

"I know it's short notice, and I appreciate you being flexible." She left the room, and he followed her out into the hallway. "I'm meeting with the contractor in thirty minutes, and I'll know more after that. I can send you a text then."

He nodded. "Of course, ma'am."

Ryan watched her leave until she turned the corner, glad she seemed more confident and less anxious than yesterday. Maybe the shock of meeting him had worn off, as she'd told him how she hadn't expected a male protection officer. He was still getting used to his principal being the youngest princess of Durham.

He figured he might as well head off to the transportation room to make arrangements for a car and driver for today and the rest of the week. Afterward, he had just enough time to research the contractor and find out where the meeting was taking place. Unless problems arose, the princess didn't have to know he'd looked into it.

Ryan arrived first at the courtyard, where Princess Emma had asked him to meet after lunch. As she came down the staircase, he couldn't keep his eyes from her.

She'd changed into a blouse with a flowery print and a pair of slacks in a blue tone that perfectly complemented her eyes. The effect was effortlessly elegant and yet mesmerizing. He snapped himself out of the admiring trance; it was out of character for him, and decidedly unprofessional.

By the time she reached him, he had recovered from his momentary slip-up and was back into proper mode.

"Good afternoon, Your Highness," he greeted her.

"Good afternoon, Mr. Sterling," she replied with a small smile.

She hadn't called him by his first name again, not after their first meeting in the small library, and his relief at that was immense. The less personal their interactions were, the better.

"Where to this afternoon, ma'am?"

"There's a home décor showroom in northern Castlebridge called Simply Home. I think I'll need a couple of hours there." She pulled out a large pair of sunglasses from her enormous purse and put them on. They effectively hid most of her face. Could she even see anything wearing the dark lenses inside?

"Very well, ma'am. If you'll just give me five minutes."

He informed the driver, then called the store manager and apprised her of Princess Emma's impending visit, apologizing for the short notice. After requesting access to a back entrance and the cooperation of the employees for a smooth experience, he returned to collect the princess, and they set out into the city.

Castlebridge on a Tuesday afternoon in late September shouldn't have been that busy, but the drive from the palace to the store took almost twenty minutes. When they arrived, the manager met them at the back and provided a store map. She offered to accompany them, but Princess Emma politely declined, thanking her for the map.

After the manager left, Princess Emma looked up from the printed map and slid the sunglasses onto her head. "I thought she would never leave." She kept her voice low.

"I was wondering myself," he admitted, in the same low tone.

She looked down to study the map again, but he caught a little smirk. "Do you think I offended her?"

"I'm sure you didn't, ma'am." If the woman got offended that easily, she had a problem.

"Can you drop the protocol while we're here?" she whispered. "It'll draw more attention if you keep ma'aming me every ten seconds."

Ryan looked around but didn't see anyone paying attention to them. He let his posture relax. "Sure, I can do that."

She nodded. "Thank you. All right. Curtains first, then fabrics, pillows, rugs, and paint last."

Somehow, he doubted she would spend only two hours looking through all that. As she started out through the store, he followed after her and, whenever the opportunity arose, positioned himself to cover her from view, trying to stay as inconspicuous as possible. Maybe tomorrow he'd wear something other than the full suit so he could blend in better and attract less notice.

The store manager approached to check on them, and Ryan had a few brief words with her before following the princess. Instead of starting in the curtains as she'd declared, Princess Emma veered to the paint section and the wall of color chips, as if unable to resist. From her large purse, she withdrew a tablet and scrolled through pictures of rooms and furniture.

She held up paint samples and turned them this way and that under the light. "Eggshell is classic, but the undertone is too yellow. Chiffon is lighter but a little cooler. What about this one? Snow. I love the blue undertone. It has a very calm vibe." She paused to study the little cards again. "What do you think?"

Was she really asking for his opinion? He'd let her ramble about colors and patterns at they'd walked through other sections of the store, not really looking at what she was doing nor really listening. His job was to keep an eye on their surroundings and warn off customers who recognized her with a steely glare. Under no circumstances would he allow anyone to approach the princess, and he made that known without a word. What did he know about tone variations of the color white? They all looked the same to him.

Another hour wore on, and Ryan noticed the effects on Princess Emma. Her shoulders drooped and she lagged, but she must also be hungry and thirsty. Should he suggest a break?

The store manager approached them again. "How is everything going, Your Highness?"

"Splendid. I'm almost done for today." Princess Emma tilted the tablet and showed the screen. "Would it be possible to get some larger samples of these fabrics?"

"Yes, of course. If you'll just follow me to my office."

As the two women discussed fabrics and paints, Ryan pulled out his phone and searched for food places nearby. What should he get—sweet or savory? Maybe sweet, as it was afternoon, only just past the traditional time for tea. Too early for a savory pre-dinner snack. He chose a pastry shop located a few blocks away, the most popular one in the city, and ordered a box with a lemon tart, a chocolate éclair, and a millefeuille, a to-go cup of sweetened mint tea, and a bottle of mineral water. After adding specific arrangements to have the order delivered to the black car parked at the back of the store, he sent a text to driver to let him know the delivery was coming.

Twenty minutes later, Princess Emma stood and thanked the manager. Ryan escorted her to the car, and she slid into the back, then he took his seat.

"Straight home, Mr. Windsor," Princess Emma said to the driver. "I'm feeling a bit peckish and need sustenance. Who knew decorating could be so tiring? What's this?" She picked up the box and opened it. "Pastries from Le Bonbon? Mr. Windsor, you're the best. And mint tea, my favorite. Thank you so much."

"You're welcome, ma'am, but thank Mr. Sterling. He ordered those," the driver replied with a hint of humor.

Ryan turned in his seat to find Princess Emma midbite with the lemon tart.

Her eyes widened, and she put down the pastry. "You did this? How?"

Ryan held up his phone. "Online ordering. I didn't know which ones you like, so I got a small selection. Hope that works, ma'am."

She nodded. "It works great. These are some of my favorites. Thank you, Mr. Sterling." She held up the box in the space between the front seats. "Please, take one. I can't eat all of these."

Both he and Mr. Windsor politely declined, and she took the box back. After taking another sip, she asked, "How did you know, Mr. Sterling?"

He caught her eyes in the rearview mirror, and the corner of his mouth lifted in a partial smile. "I thought you looked a little peckish."

Chapter Five

$\mathcal{E}$mma had underestimated the number of paint chips, fabric samples, and pictures of furniture arrangements she had to carry at any given time, especially when she met with the contractor and when she visited showrooms in the city.

On Tuesday night, she'd stayed up late organizing all the samples and pictures in a small ring-binder with divisions for each room and a separate section for the nursery. That was her special project and part of her gift for Charlotte—a theme of classic Durham fairy tales. In addition, the main wall in the nursery room would feature a hand-painted family tree of the Somerset and Montgomery lines. She also had the idea of collecting items that had belonged to Charlotte and Adam when they were babies and children to be used in the decoration. Emma's excitement grew every time she looked at the final plans. Keeping it all a secret from Charlotte would be the biggest challenge.

The week had gone by in a whirlwind of planning meetings, drives to the city, and long shopping trips. Today was Friday already, and she'd told Mr. Sterling she had to go to the mall in downtown Castlebridge where the baby store was located. Not just any baby store, but the most popular, fashionably posh one in Durham and the continent. But it wasn't the store's popularity that mattered to Emma—it also carried items of the utmost quality.

It being the start of the weekend, Mr. Sterling had asked that they leave in the morning instead of after lunch like on the days before. Emma rearranged her schedule and made plans to meet with the contractor before the end of the day. At least she had two days to catch up and pack before leaving on her trip on Monday.

As busy as this week had been, the coming one promised to be busier, and after spending more time with Mr. Sterling in the past few days than with anyone else she could remember in a long while, the trip would have them in even closer proximity.

He'd surprised her on Tuesday. That box of pastries from Le Bonbon had been completely unexpected, and her opinion of him had shifted a nudge. On Wednesday, she'd forgotten her phone, leaving it on a stack of fabric samples, and he'd returned it to her, even before she'd missed it. On Thursday, he'd had a bottle of water at the ready for her, just as she'd been wishing for one. So he was observant and had recognized her needs before she'd asked for anything; but weren't those the kind of skills a protection officer should have anyway?

Emma shoved her tablet and the binder into her purse, willing herself to stop thinking about Mr. Sterling and the little things he'd done for her all week. And here she was on Friday, wondering what kind of surprise he'd pull off today. Maybe she'd do better not to expect anything.

When they arrived at the mall, Mr. Sterling directed the driver to the underground parking. The car stopped right in front of the elevator, which they took one floor up and exited straight next to the store, as quickly as possible and away from prying eyes.

The Little Bluebird specialized in everything expectant parents needed for their new baby, or in Emma's case, for her new godchild. She pulled out the binder and walked to the furniture section, with Mr. Sterling closely following.

"Good morning, Your Highness," the store manager said. "My name is Betty. Please let me know when you're ready for assistance."

Emma nodded before continuing. "Thank you, Betty."

The displays were set up fully decorated, one each for blue and pink, and two side-by-side in neutral tones of pale green and muted yellow, interspersed with whites, creams, and grays. As fun as a gender-specific nursery would be, a neutral palette made more sense and would work better with the theme Emma had chosen.

She made a note on the margin of the sketch. Next to her, Mr. Sterling shifted again, and his masculine scent wafted her way. His proximity drove her to distraction, and she berated herself for it.

"You're doing that thing again," she said in a low voice.

His eyebrows scrunched. "What thing?"

Emma fingered the edge of a baby blanket. "The thing where you try to cover me from view every time someone moves around in the vicinity." A row of small elephant stuffed animals sat on the shelf and she smiled at them. "Also called hovering."

"It's what I do, ma'am. I hover."

She glared at him.

"Right," he said. "No ma'aming when shopping."

He turned again, and she caught sight of the dark-gray trousers and the light blue dress shirt he wore today. Sleeves rolled back and no tie made for an absolute study in sophistication and good taste. Not that she should be noticing the differences between his suit days and his dressed-down days—he looked fine either way. And she shouldn't be noticing that, either, especially about her protection officer.

What would happen if she let him hover, let others think they were a couple shopping for their baby?

Where had that rogue thought come from? She shook herself from the diversion of the imposing, muscled male beside her, the one whose presence she found herself growing accustomed to—and possibly even enjoying, were she being honest with herself. The nursery sketches awaited, and she compared them to the linen display in front of her.

Focus. She needed a big dose of it right now.

Or maybe an interruption of another sort. Emma called the store manager over, and within moments, the woman had Emma in a private consultation room, sitting down in a comfortable chair and served with a tray of midmorning snacks. Mr. Sterling had politely refused the other chair and stood aside, strategically placed behind her so that Emma could forget about him for a few minutes.

Much better.

Betty proved to have the impeccable taste and know-how to help Emma choose and order all the furniture for the baby's room, with said pieces to be delivered after the walls were painted and the mural finished, to be followed by curtains, rugs, and linens. By then, Emma would be ready to put in her own finishing touches and personal items. She was sure Charlotte would cry when she saw it, and it felt so good to do something for her cousin, who was so much more than that. They were best friends and sisters.

As she left the consultation room, Mr. Sterling approached. "How did it go, ma'am?" His voice was only loud enough for a private conversation between them, and he had the peculiar ability to stand at the edge of her personal bubble—never too far, never too close.

"Very well, thank you." Emma donned her large sunglasses, the ones that hid most of her face. If only she could hide away her heart as well as her eyes.

"Ready to head back to the car?" Mr. Sterling asked.

"Not yet. There are a couple of stores I need to visit." The chocolatier and the organic lotion and candle boutique, two of Charlotte's favorites. Emma would send her a surprise care package that would surely raise her cousin's spirits.

She entered the store and went straight to the refrigerated display cases, where rows and rows of tiny chocolates in different shapes and flavors winked brightly from behind the glass. Maybe she'd get a small box to take back with her for today; Aunt Nicolette was partial to the lavender ones.

"What's your favorite?" she asked Mr. Sterling.

He stepped closer to her and hesitated for a mere second before replying. "I don't have one."

Emma raised an eyebrow and lowered her glasses to look at him. "You don't like chocolate?"

"I do, but I haven't tried this brand."

"You should. These are the best."

He nodded, already half-turned to the customers in front of them, standing as a human shield to her.

From the corner of her eye, Emma noticed a group of girls talking in low tones among themselves. She turned her back to them, but a few minutes later, one of them approached her.

"You're Princess Emma, aren't you?" one of the three girls asked.

"Can we take a selfie with you, please?" asked another.

Before Emma had a chance to say anything, Mr. Sterling stepped in front of her and blocked her from the girls.

"Absolutely not," he said in a terse voice. "You just don't ask Her Royal Highness for a selfie. Besides being in bad taste, it's also against protocol."

"For real?" the girl at the front asked.

The lady behind the counter nodded in agreement. "He's right. Everybody knows that. Well, everyone in

Durham does. From the way you talk, you three are Americans, aren't you?"

The trio smiled wide and nodded vigorously. "We're from Idaho," one of them announced.

"That explains it," Mr. Sterling said, then added louder, "but it doesn't excuse your behavior. It's your responsibility to learn the customs of the land you visit." He kept a straight face and a stern tone. "Where are your parents?"

Emma covered a small smile with her hand. He must be overreacting on purpose.

At his question, the girls sobered from their exuberance. "We're on a school trip," said one.

"Yeah, we're high school seniors. No parents," said another one.

"Just some chaperone teachers," said the third. "But we had permission to come to the mall."

Mr. Sterling folded his arms across his chest, his biceps bunching under the fabric of his shirt. This was not the time to notice how well he looked in that shirt, not with him all serious and scolding a group of American students.

"You mean to say you're here without adult supervision?" he asked them.

The girl at the front squared her shoulders. "We don't need supervision. We're adults."

One of her friends nodded. "We're all eighteen, not little kids."

Some of them were probably younger and bluffing about their age.

"That's great, then," he said. "I don't need to inform anyone of your impending visit to the police station. I'll just call the officers to come take you."

The girls took a step back and huddled closer.

Maybe that was going too far. Emma touched Mr. Sterling's arm, and he stepped up to her, still keeping an eye on the girls.

"I think that's enough, Mr. Sterling," Emma whispered to him. "You don't need to scare them."

He dropped his arms to the side and gave her a clipped neck bow. "As you wish, Your Highness." Then, to the girls, "Her Royal Highness is a kind person and says we don't need to involve the authorities."

The girls thanked him, but he kept his grave expression. "Now let me see your phones. I know you must have sneaked some photos of Her Highness before you approached her."

"But we have rights," one of the girls protested weakly.

"Nobody will believe us without the pictures," another said.

Without uttering a word, Mr. Sterling turned his palm up, and they handed him the phones with no more objections. He deleted a couple of photos and then escorted them to the door.

The store manager apologized for the incident, and Emma assured her she had nothing to apologize for, as it hadn't been her fault.

After her purchases were finalized, they left the chocolatier, and she suggested they go home.

"You had too much fun with that, didn't you?" She couldn't resist asking him on the way to the underground garage.

"I don't know what you're talking about, ma'am." He regarded her with an innocent expression. "I was just doing my duty."

His poker face didn't fool her. He had a lighter side after all.

Chapter Six

This wasn't what Ryan had planned to do before retiring for the day.

But something in Princess Emma's expression during this afternoon's meeting had sent a warning to his gut. He always trusted his gut.

After the last four days of running errands and shopping in the city with her, he'd glimpsed a bit of her personality, had even believed he was starting to understand her. Every time she turned those unwavering blue eyes on him, his heart tripped and his chest tightened. Every single time, he fought the attraction.

But that was on him, the way he reacted to her, as if he were a fifteen-year-old kid with his first crush. He couldn't even remember the last time he'd gone out on a date; there was no time. His work was his life.

And now this.

He didn't want it to happen. It couldn't happen. Whatever *it* was, it had the potential to monumentally blow up his career plans, and he would never allow that.

Earlier today, he had called everybody for a meeting to finalize the daily calendar for the trip, despite it being Saturday. After Princess Emma's busy week with her duties, and everyone else's schedules, there hadn't been any other day that worked for everyone.

The trip was slated to start on Monday on a tight schedule. Instead of meeting with her alone in the morning, Ryan and Princess Emma had met an hour before their appointment with the social secretary, the drivers, and the other two protection officers. The princess had questioned the necessity for more agents, but once Ryan explained he'd cleared the new protocol with Mr. Peters, she hadn't said anything else about it.

Was it too much to hope she wouldn't give him any trouble? Ryan had taken Her Majesty's heeding regarding Princess Emma's independence to heart and was steeling himself to deal with her behavior, despite the lack of any signs of it during the past week.

But her earlier mention of solo outings had nagged at the back of his mind. If it was true that she was getting out of the palace by herself, and if she somehow sabotaged his looking after her, it didn't bode well for his expectations of advancement with a job well done, not to mention how her safety would be at risk.

Too many ifs.

He would keep an open mind until he found out more, but his instincts told him there might be a problem, as much as he didn't want there to be.

They had talked about her calendar and responsibilities, and then Ryan fastidiously went over every aspect of the itinerary with Mrs. Campion and Mr. Myles, the other driver, Mr. Weiss, and Protection Officers Black and Little, who were the antitheses of their names. Princess Emma tried to hide her irritation at the repetition of notes and observations, and he ignored it. Not until everyone knew their parts and what was expected of them, including Her Highness, would he be satisfied. Being prepared was imperative.

After the others left, Ryan stayed behind instead of leaving the room.

"You can go, Mr. Sterling," Princess Emma said. She stood and walked to the door. "I won't be leaving the palace today and won't need your company."

The soft look on her face came too easy, entreating him to take her words at face value, but Ryan didn't trust her innocent expression. "Very well, ma'am," he told her without pausing, without giving her a reason to doubt his agreement. "I'll see you on Monday morning."

"I'll be there," she replied too brightly.

He let her pass first, and she left toward the private royal wing where her apartment was located. Ryan watched her until she turned the corner, wishing he could figure out a way to speed up the confidence between them, knowing too well it took time, patience, and a willingness on both parts. He exhaled a pent-up breath and made his way out.

Despite his earlier efforts, he hadn't been able to get more out of her about her solo outings. Princess Emma had fielded his careful questions like an expert in handling interrogations. Maybe she was, given her upbringing.

Instead of returning to his apartment, he detoured to the security room in the administrative wing. Computer screens filled the walls, and a rotating team monitored the public spaces in the palace and the common rooms in the royal family's private wing, as well as the connecting corridors between the two.

Ryan introduced himself to the shift leader. "I'm Ryan Sterling, Princess Emma's PPO."

The man shook his hand. "I'm Charles Cain. How can I help?"

"I'd like to look at all the points where the private wing's hallways lead to the public rooms."

"I can set you up over here." Cain led Ryan to a computer in the corner, sat down, and clicked for a minute until a series of views showed up on the monitor. "Here." He stood and indicated the chair to Ryan. "These are the four exits. Just click F10 for the map view."

Ryan took the seat and set to work studying the hallways and the connecting exits. If Princess Emma was indeed sneaking out of the palace, the easiest way would be through those points that led to the public rooms. From there, she could easily blend in with visitors by disguising herself.

After spending a half hour examining the different scenarios and taking notes, Ryan thanked Cain and left. The short walk to his apartment afforded him the time to take a mental inventory of how his day had gone, a list of everything he'd set out to do and how he'd done it.

Why did he feel like something was missing?

Frustration rose for a moment. Adjusting to a new location and position was par for the course with a new job, but he didn't usually feel so out of sorts. This time, a sense of incompletion followed him after hours and rose with him in the morning. What could he do to build a relationship of trust with Princess Emma? Neither one of them had expected the current situation, but that didn't mean they couldn't make it work. He especially felt responsible for fostering an easier rapport with her, but one week of working together wasn't enough for that.

At the same time, there was a connection with the princess—an affinity that lingered in the background, one he wanted to pretend wasn't there but somehow couldn't. How to explain the way his heart sped up at the sight of her and his palms sweat? At least physical reactions were easier to manage, simple to bury behind lock and key. He wasn't the kind of person to ignore his problems, but this one was taking too much of his headspace, and that was the last thing he wanted. Not when he always strove for clean focus and faultless concentration.

A few minutes later, Ryan arrived at his apartment. He removed his suit coat and tie and rolled up his sleeves, then set up his laptop on the small kitchen table to work for a few hours. He'd obtained printouts of the reports of official visits and activities from the past year in which Princess Emma had participated, and was reading through selected dates. Though not his favorite activity, it helped him form a picture of the princess's demeanor in public. Shopping for errands in the city center didn't give him the details he needed. In addition, he also skimmed through news video footage available for some of those events. She always looked poised and elegant, notwithstanding the occasional mischievous expressions between her and her cousin Princess Charlotte during more relaxed moments.

After making a sandwich for lunch, he changed into a pair of dark jeans, black sneakers, and a graphic T-shirt of an eighties' band. With sunglasses, a baseball cap, and a broken-in backpack, he'd easily pass for a tourist. He stood in front of the mirror, assessing the overall effect. He had a hunch the princess was getting out of the palace on her own, and he planned to follow her without her knowledge, but what if it didn't work out? What if he was coming at the wrong time? Or maybe he had it all wrong and she wasn't showing up at all.

But Ryan's ability to put himself in his principal's place had served him well so far in his career, and he was counting on his instincts to be right once more—if he were Princess Emma, with less than a couple of days before an important event, he'd want some time for himself away from responsibilities. She'd be going on her solo outing, and he'd be there to witness it.

From his research of the security room's camera footage, Ryan had learned that the palace's public rooms were busier in the early afternoon. In the middle of the week, buses of tourists made up the bulk of peak hours, even this late in the summer, which was the perfect environment for someone who wanted to blend in with the visitors, as the princess did. Unless he was mistaken—and his gut told him he wasn't—Princess Emma would know how to look perfectly ordinary so as to not call any attention to herself.

Instead of heading straight to the palace, Ryan walked in the opposite direction, past the old city walls, until he reached the historical downtown area. The hot temperatures of July and August had finally abated into milder weather, and tourists abounded in the crowded streets. He took out his phone and used the camera to take a few photos, then tagged behind a large group on a guided tour making their way to the palace.

When he arrived, he bought a ticket for the public rooms and gardens, then blended with a different group to pass through the security checkpoints. He deposited his backpack on the plastic tray and emptied his pockets. As he'd only been working at the palace for a short time, he doubted he'd be recognized, especially on a day as crowded as today. Still, after removing his sunglasses, he kept a curious expression as a normal visitor would but avoided the security cameras. The palace was impressive, and he didn't have to fake his admiration.

He'd lived in Castlebridge when he was younger but had never taken the chance to visit the palace and was only familiar with the public rooms from the brief tour he'd gotten when he'd arrived at his position last month. Most visitors were interested in the throne room, but Ryan walked in the other direction, away from the audience chambers, the receiving parlors, and the north portrait gallery, until he reached the secondary corridor with its row of small offices. As he passed groups of people, the reality of the task he'd set for himself became clearer—how was he supposed to find

Princess Emma with so many visitors around? What if he was wrong about all of it?

He persisted, keeping his gaze trained on women wearing hats, caps, or scarves of any kind, eliminating people who weren't the right height or age, or those accompanied by friends or family. She would be alone; that much he knew.

After Ryan had been touring and blending in for an hour, a woman wearing a headscarf with a long tunic and fitted pants caught his eye. She wore the scarf tightly wound on her head and neck, and pulled forward so as to shield her face. Flat shoes and a small purse slung across her chest completed her outfit. In addition, she wore ear buds with the cord tucked into a pocket and carried a dictionary, pausing frequently to look up words as she read captions and small signs.

Ryan couldn't see her face, but her height and build were a match to the princess.

It had to be her.

Keeping his distance, he followed her. Slowly, she made her way back to the north gallery and took a side exit toward the gardens, always behind a large group, much as he'd done when he'd come to the palace earlier. The purposeful behavior was another indication.

Once outside, she pulled on a large pair of sunglasses that covered most of her face, a different pair from the ones the princess had worn all week. The scarf slipped, and he caught a glimpse of dark hair pulled back before she adjusted the fabric. Princess Emma had worn her hair in a low bun this morning.

Her actions became more deliberate as she followed a path away from the large crowds and eventually settled on a park bench tucked in an alcove. She sat and looked both ways, then pulled out her phone and started scrolling through it. After a few minutes, her posture visibly relaxed and a genuine smile graced her face as she paid attention to the screen. Although it never had been for him, he'd seen that smile in the past few days. She had an unmistakable smile, the kind that left an impression. What would it be like to be the recipient? To be the one who caused her to smile like that?

Ryan shook the thought but hesitated. He was about to interrupt her small moment of freedom, something that couldn't be avoided. Her safety was more important.

He turned on to a parallel path that led him to the alcove from the other direction, approached the bench, and quickly sat down on the other end of it.

Immediately, she turned away from him and fumbled with her phone before getting up.

"You're safe, Your Highness," Ryan said. "It's only me."

Chapter Seven

*E*mma froze. How had he found her?

Her shoulders slumped, and she stood with her back to him for a long second. At last, she conceded defeat and sat down again, keeping her distance.

For another moment, neither one of them said anything. She glanced at him, who was completely at ease, with an arm resting on the back of the bench and a leg crossed on the opposite knee, as if they were like any other two people visiting the gardens, instead of a Somerset and her protection officer.

He looked so different dressed in jeans and a T-shirt instead of the usual dress shirt and pants, or the full suit; she hardly recognized him. Even his hair was styled in a more relaxed fashion, transforming his appearance from the same man she'd seen only this morning. The little tug in her center pulled again, that wisp of attraction that drew her to him unwillingly. It was nothing more than a string of emotion, without reason or explanation, a faint connection that couldn't be, one she continued to ignore with resolved conviction.

But his voice had stopped her. After four full days of working together, she knew his voice already, knew how the deep rumble caused a flutter in her chest. This was definitely not the moment to let any shred of attraction flare up, not after he'd followed her in such an underhanded manner.

How in the world had he managed to find her? How did he know she would be here? Why had he done it?

Irritation filled her chest. At him for finding her, but mostly at herself for the little comment about her solo outings that had slipped unintentionally on Monday. He'd obviously latched on to it and done his research. It was her fault.

"I underestimated you, Mr. Sterling," she said.

He didn't comment.

"What are you going to do, now that you found my little secret?"

He straightened. "I had planned to turn my discovery over to Mr. Peters."

"He'll tell Aunt Nicolette."

"For sure he would, ma'am," Mr. Sterling said.

He would? "Does that mean you changed your plans?" A thread of hope made an appearance when he hesitated. "You won't say anything?"

He glanced at her. "What kind of protection officer would I be if I kept this information to myself?"

"One who's loyal to his principal," she replied immediately.

He shook his head. "Loyalty doesn't preclude duty, and it's my responsibility to keep you safe. What you're doing is the opposite of that."

Drat the man and his logic. She wanted to argue with him that she hadn't left the palace, she was still on royal grounds, but already knew he wouldn't listen.

"I'll tell him, but not today," Ryan Sterling added.

Emma turned to look at him. "I suppose you expect my gratitude for keeping your temporary silence."

"No, I expect your cooperation. Now and when the time comes." The intensity of his gaze raised a blush to her cheeks. "For the time being, we won't do anything. We're leaving on Monday and need to focus on that. I'll be able to keep an eye on you much more closely during the trip."

"Meaning, I won't have the time or opportunity to go out on my own while we're traveling." She wouldn't let that happen, not if she could help it. She had no intention to cancel the visit to the property in Hillside Meadows and she wouldn't be telling him of her plans.

This time he nodded. "That's exactly what I mean. When we return, we'll meet with Mr. Peters to deal with this."

She crossed her legs and angled her body away from him. Of all the situations to be in on her one free day, this wasn't one she had planned for. "You're not supposed to hold so much power."

"What power?" He looked perplexed.

She sat back and crossed her arms. "Power over me. It makes our relationship unbalanced." He frowned and she went on. "You're responsible for my safety, and you know my secret. I'm not even your employer, which means your job is secure."

"This is not a game, Your Highness. I'm not here to exert control over you. My job is to keep you safe, and I need your assurance that you will help me in that."

Of course he couldn't see the imbalance between them. Most likely, he'd never had to worry about his freedom, had never yearned to get away from his responsibilities. He wouldn't understand what her life was like, why she'd done this, why she needed some time for herself, even if in the literal shade of the palace.

"Do I have your promise, Princess Emma?" he insisted.

She held a firm gaze on him. "You have my word, Mr. Sterling." She swallowed the prickle of conscience at the back of her throat, the one that told her she was withholding important information from him, however small a detail. By the time he found out, it would be done, and she could explain and apologize then.

He nodded, apparently satisfied with her answer, then pulled his phone out and glanced at the screen. "Would thirty minutes be enough?"

"Enough for what?" Emma asked him.

"Would you like a half hour before returning to the private wing?"

"You mean, time by myself?" Her breath hitched, and she quickly breathed through it. "You're not going to escort me back right now?"

"I'm not taking you back by the arm, if that's what you're asking." A hint of amusement flashed through his features, but he didn't smile. "I'll leave you alone but keep you in sight and follow you back to make sure you're safe. I assume you return the same way you got out?"

She shrugged lightly. "It works." Or it had worked until today.

"Very well." He pulled his sunglasses back on, then stood. "Have a good afternoon, Your Highness."

He readjusted the backpack she hadn't noticed until now and strolled away into a merging path.

For a blessed moment, Emma was alone, no visitors milling around, no sounds but the quiet buzzing of insects and the trilling of nearby birds. In the shade of a large centennial oak, and shielded from the city noise, she could almost believe herself to be somewhere else entirely different—out in the countryside, in an alternate reality.

She sat back and relaxed her shoulders and tipped up her face to the smell of grass and flowering bushes that bloomed late into the season, the leaves rustling in the stately trees.

A brief respite.

Too soon, a group of foreign tourists and their guide interrupted her break. It was time to return anyway. She stood and looked around but didn't find Mr. Sterling lurking behind the trees, although she didn't doubt he was nearby, as he'd said he'd be.

On Monday morning, Emma zipped her suitcase and set it by the front door of her apartment. It held two official outfits for each day with matching shoes and accessories. These were the clothes and shoes that had been carefully selected under the supervision of the royal stylist, Mrs. Keeling, and Emma would be wearing them in public for the official visits. Every item had been nitpicked in meticulous detail. A list had been typed and pictures sent to her phone, as if she would forget. Yes, it was Emma's first solo visit, and she was representing the king and queen of Durham, but it was in her personal interest to appear at her best and above reproach, and not just for the sake of the crown. She'd even had a brush-up lesson on deportment and decorum that would have made Mrs. Grant—the decorum tutor Emma and Charlotte had had growing up—proud.

The small leather purse she carried today sat on her bed and her large bag lay open next to it as she decided what else to bring with her. At the bottom, and in preparation for her side trip, she'd already added a pair of sneakers, jeans, a sweater, and a hoodie. She couldn't very well wear her official wardrobe to lounge at the hotel in between appearances, even less for her unscheduled detour.

When her phone rang with the ringtone assigned to Charlotte, Emma answered the video call.

"I know you're on your way out," Charlotte said, "but I wanted to wish you good luck before you left."

"I have a few minutes," Emma said, sitting down on the side of the bed. "Just trying to decide what I really need to take with me."

"What are you wearing?"

Emma angled the camera to give her cousin a better view of her outfit. "Black trousers and a blouse for the trip. I'll change into a dress for my first visit."

"Which dress?"

"The navy one with white polka dots."

"You'll look so elegant, Emma. Remind me again of your itinerary."

"Edenshire today, Meeds tomorrow, a day off on Wednesday, and Inverly on Thursday, the last day."

"That's right. I remember now," Charlotte said. "That's quite the circuit for your first trip by yourself."

Emma winced. "I hope I don't mess it up."

"Of course you won't. You've done this before, and you're fabulous at it."

"Not by myself, I haven't. The few times we went, it was always with your parents or the boys."

"It's not much different. Just pretend one of us is standing behind you. Only this time you don't have to deal with the boys making faces."

Emma chuckled. "Just pray I won't be overrun by nerves and forget protocol."

"Do you have any scheduled stops in between the official visits?" Charlotte asked.

"As few as possible and meticulously mapped. Mr. Sterling is very strict." Except for the third day on the trip, when Emma planned to keep her appointment to see the property during the day off. But something held her from telling Charlotte her plans right now. When she returned, she would make a full account to her cousin.

"You're back to calling him Mr. Sterling?"

"Using his first name is not going to work," Emma replied. "It would be awkward if I slipped in public." She didn't have the time to tell Charlotte about him discovering her secret on Saturday. Come to think of it, Charlotte didn't know of Emma's little escapades by herself, and now was not the time to confess.

Before Charlotte had a chance to comment, Emma stood from the bed and turned the camera around to show the items lying on the bed. "Tell me what I really need to take, Char."

They weeded through Emma's pile until the necessities were packed in her overnight bag and then said goodbye.

When Emma descended the staircase that led to the private courtyard, she found Aunt Nicolette and Uncle Geoffrey waiting for her at the bottom.

"This is a surprise," Emma said with a smile.

"We wanted to wish you good luck, Emma dear," Aunt Nicolette said.

How did they know she needed the encouragement?

"The first solo trip is always nerve inducing," Uncle Geoffrey said, as he and Aunt Nicolette accompanied Emma to the door.

"Maybe just a little," Emma admitted.

"Jitters are normal," Aunt said. "Have confidence in yourself, Emma. We know you'll do well."

One of the valets took her overnight bag and opened the door.

"In the back seat, please," Emma instructed. She definitely wanted the overnight bag at her feet for easy access to her tablet and whatever else she might need.

Aunt Nicolette brought Emma in for a hug, and Uncle Geoffrey laid his arm over her shoulders for a side hug, and they said their goodbyes. Emma pulled on her sunglasses, slipped her arm through her handbag, and stepped outside. Three black sedans with heavily tinted windows were parked in a row and already turned toward the courtyard's exit.

Mr. Sterling stood by the middle car, his hands crossed in front of him, his posture erect. At the sight of him in a dark-gray suit, Emma's heart skipped a beat. The flash of attraction surprised her again, and she quickly tamped it down as if it hadn't happened. A rogue feeling—nothing more. Never mind the other rogue feelings before this one; it wasn't a pattern.

When she approached, he squared his shoulders and opened the back passenger door for her. "Good morning, Your Highness."

"Good morning, Mr. Sterling. Are we ready to leave?" Inane question, as she could see they were.

"Yes, ma'am. Mr. Weiss is at the ready for us. Mr. Myles and Mrs. Campion are waiting in the car behind, and Officers Black and Little in the one in front."

Emma slid into the seat and smoothed the side of her black trousers, willing herself to calm down.

Mr. Sterling shut the door, took the seat next to the driver, and then turned to look at her. "Don't forget your seat belt, please."

"Yes, of course." Emma fumbled with the latch, trying to fasten it as quickly as possible and taking longer than it warranted instead. At last she was done, palms sweaty, cheeks warm with lingering embarrassment. Not a good start. "Thank you for the reminder."

He nodded at the driver, and after some kind of signal to the other cars, they pulled away, exited the palace courtyard, and soon merged into the city traffic.

Ready or not, she was doing this.

Chapter Eight

Ryan caught Princess Emma's reflection in the rearview mirror.

She'd seemed nervous when they met this morning, and, for a moment, he'd feared she'd hold a grudge for his interference with her walk in the palace gardens on Saturday. When he'd greeted her with a small smile, she'd returned it with one of her own, and relief washed through him. Was it genuine or for the benefit of the king and queen watching from the door? He hoped the former. They would be working together much closer for the next few days, and keeping a good relationship with her was important to him. It could make or break the tone of the trip.

The travel appeared to have relaxed her. Following a two-hour drive, they'd arrived at Edenshire and had checked in at the same hotel that had served the royal party for the last visit some years back. The staff were discreet and experienced in dealing with security for the celebrities they often hosted, and the accommodations had the right blend of comfort and elegance.

After a lunch in the privacy of her room and an hour to rest and change, they were now en route to the first visit, a public school and after-hours activity center for underprivileged children. The second visit was to the pediatric wing at the local hospital where Princess Emma was scheduled to meet with children and their families and pose for pictures with them, as well as with hospital and city officials. The second day was even more packed with appearances, and he was glad for the break on the third day.

So far, everything was going according to plan and they were making good time. Even the weather held to predictions: partly cloudy and mild, with light showers and cooling temperatures in the forecast for the rest of the week. Not that it made much difference since all the visits were indoors, but Ryan didn't like surprises. As their travels took them farther north and closer to the Atlantic, this time of year brought more chances of inclement weather, and he'd keep an eye on the forecast app in the remote case that they had to readjust their routes. It was always safer to be prepared.

In the back seat, Princess Emma had her eyes trained on her phone and her thumbs flying on the screen keyboard, a playful pull tugging at the corners of her mouth. Was she talking to a friend? Whoever it was, she looked at ease, almost happy. How many close friends did she even have, other than her family?

What did he know of her private life? Not much, if he thought about it. Only what was pertinent for him to do his job. He was curious, of course, but he didn't let the curiosity linger. At least, not for now. In time, he'd find out more about her. It was bound to happen the longer he spent in her company.

Up ahead, Black and Little pulled up to a side street. Ryan brought his attention back from the princess and focused on the surroundings.

They entered the school through a side door, with Officer Black in the front, Mrs. Campion to Princess Emma's right, Ryan immediately behind to her left, and Little bringing up the rear a few yards behind. Some of the journalists were allowed inside the school, but only a few, much to Ryan's relief. The media always complicated things.

In the main hallway, the school director did a small curtsy when Princess Emma approached. "Welcome, Your Royal Highness. It is an honor to have you."

After a walk through the main hallway, the princess peeked into some classrooms, the library and media room, the kitchen and the cafeteria, and ended in the gymnasium that also doubled as the assembly room.

There, the school choir sang to Princess Emma, and a first-grade girl curtsied and presented a handmade book with drawings and messages from the students. The princess crouched to the girl's level and looked her in the eyes, as if no one else mattered. She conversed with the child for a few minutes and even knelt on the floor in an outfit that was clearly not made for it. After, she stood and thanked the students, teachers, and staff for their hard work, posed for some pictures, and they left. Short and sweet.

From the school, they drove directly to the hospital. Edenshire was the largest town in the county but not a large city by normal standards, with a population of fifty-five thousand, so the local hospital served the surrounding communities as well. From what he'd learned, the pediatric wing had recently been opened with funds from a royal endowment. Princess Emma was here today to visit the new facilities, represent Her Majesty the queen, and pose for official pictures.

After the usual protocol for arrivals, the hospital director took the princess to the new wing. Every time she went in one of the hospital rooms to greet a child, too many people followed her in, overwhelming the children and making it impossible to exchange anything but a few words with the parents. Although she kept a smile, Ryan noticed the strain in her eyes at the others crowding the space. Maybe there was something he could do to help with that.

In one of the rooms, a child in a wheelchair caught Princess Emma's attention. Something passed in her expression, but she smiled nonetheless, effectively hiding the compassion and putting on a brave face and cheerful voice when she approached the little boy. She gave him all her attention, that touch of magic that made the child feel like the most important person in the world, his smile sparking with joy. He held up a tattered stuffed animal, and she patted the toy without hesitation.

Wistfully, he thought back to his own childhood. What would it have been like to have someone kind and gentle like her take even a few minutes for him back then? How much of a difference would it have made?

She looked happy and at ease. If he hadn't seen how nervous she'd been this morning, he'd think she did this often. Throughout the day, he witnessed the transformation from the stressed, self-conscious woman to this generous person centered on giving as much as possible of her undivided attention to the children she met. By now, her hair had slipped from its perfect coiffure, and her outfit didn't look as pristine as it had in the beginning, but she was obviously not concerned with any of that.

Knowing it was her first solo appearance, he was even more impressed. Her smile was genuine, and her interaction with the children and families had been warm and authentic, giving her attention to each one in turn. He hadn't expected her to behave any differently, but he hadn't counted on seeing first hand how much she cared for each person she met, especially the children. Ryan almost wished he could tell her what a good job she'd done, but he wouldn't, of course. It wasn't his place to compliment her, and there were certain boundaries he didn't want to cross.

How did she really feel about her duties and responsibilities? If she weren't a royal, might she have been a teacher, or even a nurse? How different would her personal life be? Maybe she would have been married by now, with a child or two of her own.

Did she even have a boyfriend? Or had one in the past? How did someone in her position even meet a guy and have a normal relationship? Come to think of it, her brother and cousins had, so it stood to reason she could too. Would he be the one tasked with protecting the princess and her significant other? Somehow, the idea of tailing after them didn't appeal to him.

Ryan shook his head—he was getting ahead of himself.

Outside the hospital's main door, the photographers waited for Princess Emma to arrive with the hospital officials and the city's mayor. Ryan and Little stepped to the side as the group posed for pictures. Despite the rain, there was a small crowd, holding Durham flags and posters with Princess Emma's name, and she smiled wide and waved at the people.

When the cars pulled up, Black exited the one at the front and approached to clear the way. Ryan stepped closer to the princess and made sure he was in her line of view.

"Your car is ready, ma'am," he said in a low voice.

She nodded at him.

He took the umbrella from Mrs. Campion and opened it over the princess's head to escort her to their car. As she stepped onto the wet pavement, her shoes slipped, and his free hand shot out to grab her elbow firmly.

She gasped, then looked up at him. They stood much closer than he'd realized, shoulder to shoulder under the privacy of the umbrella, rain still pounding around them.

"Thank you," she whispered. Her gaze held his momentarily before she turned her attention to the ground.

Ryan let go of her arm. "Of course, ma'am."

He opened the back door for her, waited until she was safely inside, then closed the door. He collapsed the umbrella and took his seat at the front.

Black's voice came over Ryan's communication device. "Ready?"

Ryan nodded to Mr. Weiss, who let go of the parking brake and made his way out to the street. "Ready," he answered.

Between his seat and the passenger door, Ryan let his hand fall and relax from the tight fist he'd been holding, then slowly wiped the sheen of moisture off his palm on his trousers.

That was the last thing he wanted, this friction of interest toward the princess.

It wasn't attraction—only curiosity.

Nothing more.

Chapter Nine

$\mathcal{E}$mma's phone rang, rousing her from a deep sleep. She fumbled for it and failed to grab it from its usual spot.

Gingerly, she cracked an eye open and, at the lack of familiar surroundings, went up on an elbow to look around. Through the partially open blinds and the pale light of an early morning outside, she distinguished the room's features and finally remembered she was at the hotel in Edenshire.

The phone rang again, and this time she grabbed it, pressing the talk button to answer her cousin. "Charlotte, this better be good. It's five in the morning." She flopped back down on the mattress.

"Sorry, Emma. I know it's early, but I think you need to see this."

At Charlotte's serious tone, Emma sat up and turned on the lamp on the bedside table. "See what?"

"I'm sending you the link."

Emma clicked on it and brought up the article. She frowned at the picture at the top, at the sight of Ryan Sterling and herself under the umbrella when they were leaving the hospital in Edenshire the day before. He'd helped steady her after she'd slipped on the rainy pavement. It had all happened so fast, she couldn't believe the photographers had caught the moment.

Her expression fell at the headline below—*Princess Emma and her new bodyguard: how cozy are they?*

A sound escaped Emma, half disgust, half gasp.

"Are you okay, Em?" Charlotte asked.

Emma clicked away from the article, not wanting to read any more. "It was nothing like this. I slipped, and he caught me before I fell down. It was so quick, it barely lasted a second."

"I believe you," Charlotte said. "I only told you so you wouldn't be caught unaware."

"Thank you. I appreciate that." It would have been worse if she didn't know. "They made it look like we were gazing into each other's eyes, like it was a private moment."

"I'm sorry."

"Stupid reporters. They always mess everything up. Why didn't they focus on the children I visited, or on the hospital workers, or so many other things that are so much more deserving of attention?"

"If it's any consolation, it's not the *Castlebridge Times*. It's only the *Daily Gazette*. They have a reputation for publishing gossip. Everyone knows that."

Emma shook her head. "What is your mother going to say when she sees this?"

Charlotte chuckled lightly. "I doubt she'll say anything. Alex and Libby trained her well."

For a few minutes, they reminisced about all the times cousin Alex and his American fiancée, now wife, had been targeted by the media, much to Aunt Nicolette's consternation.

"What are you going to do?" Charlotte asked.

"Nothing for now, unless it becomes more of an issue. If I pretend it didn't happen, it'll lose the appeal. The less attention I give to it, the less important it becomes."

"You're right. That's a good plan. By the way, you said Mr. Sterling reminded you of James Kinnaird, and I can see what you mean. There's a definite resemblance."

"You see it too?" Emma asked.

"I'll never say anyone is more attractive than James K., but your new protection officer is a close second."

Emma was well aware how attractive Ryan Sterling was.

"He's movie star dashing," Charlotte continued.

"You're exaggerating, Char."

"I'm just teasing. You know I only have eyes for Adam."

"And he only has eyes for you." Emma always felt like the proverbial third wheel around her cousin and her husband, for how in love with each other they were.

Charlotte's voice lowered, with a smile evident in her tone. "I know. He's so great."

"Yes, he is," Emma agreed, then yawned. "Excuse me."

"I woke you up too early. I better let you go."

"Thanks for calling and letting me know."

"You're welcome. Good luck today."

They said goodbye and hung up.

Emma put the phone back on the bedside table and lay down in bed. Even as she tried to fall asleep, her mind turned round and round with the picture she'd seen of her and Ryan, with the news link and the headline, with Charlotte's comments. Though her eyes were tired, the pull of the candid photo was too great. Emma retrieved her phone from the nightstand and opened the link Charlotte had sent.

She studied Ryan's face—there it was, she was thinking of him by his first name again—and was surprised at the look he gave her. It mirrored hers—which was startled, and not in an I-almost-fell sort of way. What had surprised her was his touch and the surge of warmth that had flown through her, jolted her almost, in the most pleasant manner. Had he felt it too? Was it even possible—

Emma dismissed the thought as quickly as it had come. There was no way that professional Ryan Sterling would allow himself to feel anything toward her—other than a responsibility to keep her safe.

She was the one with the problem. And now the media had just made it so much worse.

She shook her head, scolding herself.

Just because he was broad-shouldered and cut a good figure in a suit didn't mean she could spare him a second glance, or third. Absolutely not.

How was she going to keep herself calm and cool beside him for the rest of the day during the official visits in the city of Meeds? Knowing the photographers were waiting for some kind of moment between her and Mr. Sterling didn't help at all.

The good news was, the trip was practically halfway done. They would be traveling to Meeds later this morning, where she would visit another school and hospital. Tomorrow was a down-day for everyone, a day to rally and rest before the visits in Inverly and the trip back to Castlebridge on Friday after lunch.

Hopefully, Aunt Nicolette didn't have more trips planned for a while. If Emma spent all her time at the palace, she wouldn't need Mr. Sterling to follow her around. That would take care of her appreciation for his broad shoulders.

That was a good plan. A minor plan.

Emma had other plans, the kind that didn't involve anyone else.

After showering and getting ready for the day, Emma was brought breakfast in her suite. She took a cup of almost-too-hot latte and sipped on it by the double doors. It had rained all night, the sound of it against the double-paned glass impossible to disregard, but the rain was harder now, more insistent and demanding, and she couldn't help the shudder that ran through her.

Mrs. Campion arrived to go over the schedule for the day, more of a formality than a necessity, and Emma revised her wardrobe plan while the lady droned on.

A knock sounded at the door. Mrs. Campion paused her narrative and looked up expectantly.

"Come in," Emma said.

Mr. Sterling passed through and bowed from the neck at her. "Good morning, Your Highness." He nodded at Mrs. Campion. "Excuse the interruption."

Emma nodded back, still holding on to her cup. She'd been trying so hard not to think of him, and here he was, already dressed for the day in a suit. His expression was the same as always—unperturbed, completely in control, not giving away whatever he was thinking about. Last Friday, he'd shown a bit of his personality when he'd dealt with the American girls, but this week he behaved too properly.

Where had this annoying attraction for him come from? He was good looking, she wouldn't deny that, but there was something more she didn't want to explore right now.

His stance was wide, his hands crossed in front of him. If he'd seen the article with the picture of them under the umbrella, he didn't show it—he looked the same as always.

Mrs. Campion cleared her throat lightly, and Emma promptly recovered. "Yes, Mr. Sterling?"

"Due to the weather conditions, we'll be departing an hour earlier than previously scheduled. I apologize for the inconvenience, Your Highness."

Emma stared at him for a moment, at a loss for words. He was only informing her of the change, nothing else, and of course, she wouldn't oppose him.

She glanced toward the bedroom door, calculating how quickly she could finish her packing, then walked over to the coffee table and deposited her cup. "Thank you, Mr. Sterling. I'll get on packing right away."

He dipped his head into a quick bow and left.

Emma got a glimpse of Protection Officer Little in the hallway before Mr. Sterling closed the door behind him. Officers Black and Little took turns on guard duty when she was at the hotel until she retired for the night. During her official visits, one of them took the front and the other took the back, with Emma and Mrs. Campion in the middle and Ryan Sterling as her sideways shadow.

She was still not completely used to having him follow her like this, and it would take some time. His scent was different, more masculine, and even his body heat radiated strength, so different from the kind she'd been used to with Lisa. His presence unsettled her—yet not in a bad way. She felt safe, and so aware of him. After so many years of Charlotte beside her, with either Karla or Lisa, or both, behind them, it was hard to come to terms with the change.

Almost an hour later, Emma and her small entourage in the three cars left the hotel in Edenshire and got on the road to Meeds, two hours to the north. The rain didn't abate and only added more time to the trip, and they would have been late if Mr. Sterling hadn't had the forethought to leave earlier.

Meeds was the largest of the three cities on Emma's itinerary, another place she had never traveled to. As they wound through the streets on the way to the hotel, she thought wistfully of warm summer days and sunny skies, instead of the gray sheets of rain and colorless cityscape before them. A visit in the late spring would be so much nicer, what with the coastline beyond and the rows of cottages perched to the east.

"Is this normal weather for the season, do you know?" she asked.

"There's a storm coming from the south, ma'am," Mr. Sterling said, then glanced at her over his shoulder. "I'm keeping an eye on it."

Emma looked outside the window before turning to him. "More than this?"

"It's possible, yes."

Should they be worried about the weather?

Mr. Weiss pulled under an awning at the back of the hotel. "We've arrived, Your Highness."

Due to delays caused by the weather, she had less time to change than the day before, and they made their way to the hospital as soon as she was ready.

When Emma stepped out of the elevator on the second floor of the hospital, her expression widened in a smile. Everywhere she looked, bright colors and large animal wall art stood in immediate contrast with the gloomy weather. Despite the fact that they were in a pediatric wing for children with serious, even life-threatening, illnesses, there was a lightness here, an effort to lend warmth and tenderness where none came by naturally.

The pediatric chief of staff walked beside her with a running commentary about numbers that didn't mean much to her. Emma was more interested in the children and their families, in the nurses who served them, and everyone else who carried the day-to-day responsibilities at the hospital. What did it matter if they were at 52 percent of their quota for the fiscal year? People were always more important, especially here.

As she passed through a room, she caught a view of a small boy sitting up in bed, alone. Doubling back, she went in and greeted him.

"Are you here to read to me?" He went on, before she could reply, "Mom couldn't visit today because of the weather, but she called and said a nice lady would come read to me, and you're the nicest lady I've seen all day."

Emma smiled. How could she say no to him? "Yes, I'm here to read to you." She pulled a chair closer to his bed.

Mrs. Campion cleared her throat. "Your Highness, the hospital director and the other gentlemen—"

"Tell them I'll be along shortly, Mrs. Campion. They can wait a few minutes."

Mrs. Campion nodded and left swiftly.

Emma turned to the boy. "My name is Emma. What's your name?"

He extended his little hand to her. "Hello, Emma. My name's Oliver."

Emma shook his fingers, enchanted with his manners. "Such a great name. I have a brother named Oliver."

"Is he a good brother?"

"He's the best kind of big brother," she said.

Oliver pointed at the door. "Who's he?"

Emma turned around in her chair to find Mr. Sterling standing at the door's opening, with a small crowd behind him. "That's Mr. Sterling. He's my—he's making sure we're safe," she said to Oliver, then addressed Mr. Sterling. "I'm not ready yet."

"That's not a problem, Yo—"

"Emma," she interrupted him. "You can call me Emma."

Amusement flashed in his eyes. "Take your time, Emma. They'll wait."

A thrill passed through her at the way he said her name.

She nodded at him before turning to Oliver again. "Tell me, what would you like me to read?" She gestured at the basket full of books on another chair.

"None of those. They're for little kids," Oliver said. "I got one here about volcanoes."

For the next ten minutes, Emma read to Oliver, willingly ignoring everything else but the interaction with the boy.

Out of the corner of her eye, she was aware of Mr. Sterling, who remained at the door, blocking the intrusion of photographers, and a spark of gratitude warmed her chest.

Later, when he escorted her to her hotel room, she called him back. "Mr. Sterling, thank you for what you did back there." At his raised eyebrow, she continued. "In the little boy's room at the hospital." How had he known she needed that time with the boy, both for Oliver's sake and hers?

"You're welcome, Your Highness." He hesitated for a fraction of a second. "I figured you needed the break and the boy needed the company."

Her eyes widened at his accurate assessment, and he frowned lightly.

"Was I wrong?" he asked.

She shook her head. "No, no. You were right. That was exactly what I wanted."

His expression relaxed. "Have a good night, Your Highness."

"One more thing, Mr. Sterling."

He waited.

Emma took a breath and released it slowly, trying to let go of the awkwardness. "I'm sure you're aware of the picture the *Daily Gazette* posted."

His gaze softened with understanding. "Yes, ma'am, I am."

"I think it's best we pretend it didn't happen. Then the media will move on."

He nodded. "That's a wise decision." After a pause, he asked, "Will that be all, ma'am?"

"Yes, thank you. Good night, Mr. Sterling."

He said good night again and closed the door behind him.

Emma stood in the middle of the room for another minute, still making sense of his ability to know her so acutely when she'd been at the hospital.

A quick knock sounded at the door.

"Who is it?" she asked, not expecting anyone this late.

"It's Ryan Sterling, ma'am. Did you lock your door?"

"Not yet."

Was he going to stay there until she locked it?

"I'll wait here until you do," he said.

Now he was a mind reader too?

She walked to the door and turned the bolt once. "Better?"

"Much. Thank you."

She plastered her ear to the door and heard him say good night to Mr. Black.

Did Ryan Sterling do this every night—wait for her to lock the door before he left to his bedroom?

Chapter Ten

When the alarm went off in the early morning, Ryan rolled out of bed and sat on the edge of the mattress. He scrubbed a hand over his face, the overnight whiskers reminding him he needed a clean shave before they left Meeds tomorrow.

After leaving Princess Emma safely inside behind her locked door last night, he'd been too wired to sit in his bedroom, let alone go to bed. Two days of car rides and official visits hadn't given him the physical exercise he needed, so he'd changed into shorts and a tank top and went to the hotel's gym to use the weight machines.

One hour of pushing himself had felt good, and focusing on the rotations and repetitions had cleared his mind of thoughts of Princess Emma. Two days of following her closely on her assignment had him spending more mental energy on her than he should. She was his principal—that wouldn't be changing anytime soon. But his job was to protect her—not to wonder what kind of books she read in her free time. Watching her read to the boy at the hospital had put all kinds of ideas in his mind.

Ryan reached for his phone and checked the Google alerts for Princess Emma's name, including any variants. He didn't want to repeat the surprise of finding his face plastered next to hers all over the internet. She said it was best to pretend it hadn't happened, but of course he thought about it. He couldn't put it out of his mind, especially how everyone had seen it as well. Having his picture taken and occasionally showing up in the press came with the job of protecting high-profile clients, but he was supposed to be in the background, not at the same level as his principal. Fortunately, he was mostly absent from the pictures covering Her Highness's visit to Meeds, as he should be.

What would she be doing today? She didn't have any visits. In fact, she didn't have anything on her schedule. He'd thought it strange, but she'd insisted on everyone having a day off before the visits in Inverly and the trip back to Castlebridge. Maybe he'd check on her later to see if she'd changed her mind, but with the weather still so rainy, a day indoors might be a good idea for everyone.

He walked to the window and drew the curtains open. Sunrise was a few minutes away, and the rain had slowed down to a steady, solid drizzle. A run would be good, even if he got soaked in the process.

After downing a packet of electrolytes in a glass of water, he dropped to the carpet and did his morning routine of sit-ups and push-ups, increasing the reps until he felt the burn.

A few minutes later, clad in sweat pants and a zip hoodie, he left his bedroom and made his way to the street-level exit at the back of the hotel. He took the service stairs down, intent on avoiding anyone who might use the elevator, and paused to stretch his muscles at the landings between each floor. Maybe he'd go visit the swimming pool when he returned from his run. He might as well take advantage of the day off and catch up on his physical training.

The back of the hotel formed a half moon to one side with a delivery dock to the other, a sidewalk running the perimeter of a wide alley that led to the front of the building.

Ryan straightened to his full height and adjusted his hoodie as he looked around the area from behind the tinted glass door. To his left, two hotel workers unloaded a small truck. To the opposite side, a woman stood under the cover of a recessed door, holding an umbrella. Something about her posture made him pause. She wore a knit cap over her head, partially covering blonde hair that barely touched her shoulders. Her skin was pale, and her eyes hid behind a pair of aviators, despite the dreariness of the morning light.

He relaxed. For a second, he'd thought it was Princess Emma waiting outside. But Her Highness was upstairs in her suite, most likely still sleeping.

A crazy, nagging impulse had him pulling out his phone. He tapped a quick message.

Your Highness, will you be needing my assistance today?

Ahead, the woman removed her phone out of a pocket, looked at the screen, then balanced the umbrella to use both her thumbs.

Ryan's phone pinged with an incoming message.

No, Mr. Sterling, I won't be needing anything today. Enjoy your day off.

His eyes snapped to the woman across the street. It couldn't be a coincidence, could it? He didn't believe in those.

A blue midlevel sedan entered from the opposite side, slowly following the crescent along the curb. The woman waved at the driver and stepped closer to the edge of the sidewalk.

Ryan's stomach dropped as he realized her intent, and he started running toward the car. He had to stop her, whomever she turned out to be. He had to make sure it wasn't the princess.

"What are you doing?" he called out loudly, reaching the back of the car at the same time she opened the door.

She froze.

Up close, he recognized her. Even behind her disguise of makeup that made her skin appear lighter and a short blonde wig, he knew her facial features.

"Where are you going?" he asked the princess.

"I need to go, Mr. Sterling." She held on to the car's door and looked up at him. "Pretend you didn't see me."

"Absolutely out of the question," he said immediately, keeping the same low tone she did.

"Please," she persisted. "I need to make it there today."

The driver turned back in his seat toward Princess Emma. "Miss, is this guy bothering you? Do you need me to call someone for help?"

She held Ryan's gaze for a long second, but he kept his expression firm. After a tense moment between them, she put on a smile and leaned inside. "I'm okay, thank you. I know him."

"Are you sure?" the man asked.

"I'm sure, and I'm so sorry for the inconvenience. How much do I owe you?"

Ryan couldn't see her face, but her voice sounded light—how she managed that, he couldn't guess—and he hoped the driver wouldn't call anyone. That was the last thing they needed.

He waited next to the open door while she settled her bill and then sent the car on its way. Princess Emma remained on the street, watching the car until it disappeared from view.

"I can't believe you stopped me from going," she said at last, facing him with a frown and a hard expression in her eyes as she removed the sunglasses.

"Of course I stopped you." Wherever she was trying to go, she couldn't go by herself. Why did she have a hard time understanding this?

"I would have been back just after lunch, maybe even earlier."

The dockworkers had stopped to look at them.

"Come on, let's talk about this inside," Ryan said.

She stalked ahead of him, and he easily caught up to her. As he held the door for her to pass inside, he reached for her elbow but quickly dropped his hand. She surely wouldn't want his fingers on her, and he didn't have a reason to touch her. His protective instincts were always at attention, but this wasn't the moment to use them. His presence alone was enough right now.

At the service elevator, they joined a maid pushing a large cart full of linens and cleaning supplies, and kept to the opposite corner as they went up. Ryan strategically stepped to Princess Emma's side to block her from the maid's view, just in case the woman saw through the disguise.

Once inside Princess Emma's suite, she walked to the double glass doors and stood there, shoulders rigid, arms folded, walls up around her like never before.

Ryan took a breath in and let it out slowly. "We need to talk, ma'am, but I'm dripping on the carpet, and so are you. Let's continue this after changing into dry clothes."

Maybe by then the right words would come to him. What could he say to convince her they had to work together? He wasn't her enemy.

She nodded, still holding her arms tightly crossed over her chest.

Ryan walked to the door, but then walked back. "I'll need your phone, ma'am."

She turned about to face him, eyes wide. "You don't trust me?"

He raised an eyebrow at her. "Give me one good reason why I should."

She blushed and cast her eyes down, then wordlessly extended her phone to him.

It surprised him that she didn't even try to argue; she must have felt guiltier than he suspected.

"I'll be back in a few minutes." He slipped the phone into his pocket and left her suite, then waited until she locked the door.

He needed time to calm down. Right now, he felt like screaming at her, with the hope that the ranting would knock some sense into her head.

Once in his bedroom, Ryan rubbed his jaw and let his posture drop. Maybe taking away Princess Emma's phone wasn't the best way to deal with the situation right now—he knew it wasn't—but she'd broken his trust again, and he wasn't willing to give her a second chance just yet.

Not until she earned it.

Chapter Eleven

*E*mma shed her puffy coat and ripped the hat off her head, then tossed them on the sofa with all the angry energy she had coursing through her. Curse Ryan Sterling and his high moral compass, his scruples, and his work ethic. Did he have to do everything by the book, follow every little rule, procedure, and protocol?

She was a Somerset, but not in direct line to the throne, and the public never fussed about her, not the way they did for her cousins. So what if she took a side trip to go check a property she was interested in buying?

She'd planned her trip to Hillside Meadows so well. Nothing had been left to chance. If not for him, she would have made it there and back without anyone's knowledge.

But, once again, her luck had been conspicuously missing in action, and he'd caught her, even while she was wearing a disguise that should have been foolproof.

Dumb blonde wig.

In the bathroom, Emma removed the wig and the skullcap, exposing her own hair, all matted down. She slipped off the elastic holding the ponytail, brushed her hair, and braided it out of the way. Then she scrubbed her face clean of the heavy makeup she'd done for her disguise, not caring to reapply anything else.

With her hoodie pulled down over her forehead and the oversize sunglasses, nobody would have recognized her, not in the dark jeans and puffy coat, so different from the way she always dressed in public. Despite what Ryan Sterling said, it was a good disguise, and the people she'd passed hadn't known it was her.

But he had. Even yards away. He'd taken a look at the woman waiting for the rideshare car and somehow known it was her.

Emma's shoulders slumped. It was wrong to resent him; she knew that. He was only doing his job, and she had promised she wouldn't make it harder.

And she'd done the opposite.

Not purposefully, but she had nonetheless. And although her reason was a good one, she didn't expect him to understand, knew he wouldn't make an effort to understand. To him, she was only the principal he had to keep safe and protected. Nothing else mattered.

She changed from her wet clothes into dry ones—another pair of jeans and a sweater—then walked to the living room to wait for Mr. Sterling.

He knocked a few minutes later, and she opened the door to him. He wore jeans and a longsleeve sweatshirt, just like any regular guy. Not the usual dark suit, and not the running clothes she'd seen him in this morning. His hair was combed and slightly wet, either from the rain outside or a quick shower, and his face remained unshaved, lending him a scruffy look she found more attractive than she ought to.

Enough with the attraction already. She was mad at him.

Emma sat on one of the sofas flanking a small coffee table, and she indicated the other one across from her to him.

Before sitting down, he returned her phone, and she set it face down next to her on the sofa. He watched her for a moment, and she resisted the urge to fidget, nearly convinced he could see through her. How did he do that? In the gray light through the curtains, his brown eyes had a depth of feeling that almost let her see him, the man and not the protection officer. But the impression didn't last long.

"I have a question for you, and I hope you'll be honest," he started.

"I'll try," she said. She wouldn't promise; she'd done that before and it hadn't worked.

"If Lisa Allen were your protection officer still, what would you have done?"

His question surprised her. "What do you mean?" She knew what he meant, but wanted to buy herself some time.

"Would you have gone behind her back, or would you have asked her to drive you?"

From his resigned tone of voice, it seemed he already knew the answer as well.

"I would have asked her to drive me," Emma admitted.

"Then why didn't you ask me?"

"I didn't think you'd understand." How could he, free to go wherever he wanted, free to do what he liked?

"Try me," he said softly. "I'm not your enemy, Your Highness. We can work together and help each other. I need to be able to do my job to keep you safe, but that doesn't mean I can't help you get as much freedom as you're permitted to have. I'm not in your life to make it harder."

Could it be that simple?

"I didn't set out to lie to you on purpose," she said.

"I believe that, but you didn't trust me either."

He had a point, but she didn't want to concede it so easily.

"Where were you going?" he asked.

"I have an appointment with a land agent to see a property in Hillside Meadows."

He pulled out his phone, most likely to look up where the place was.

She glanced at the time on the screen of her phone. "Well, had an appointment, I should say."

"The appointment was this early?"

"No, but I won't be making it anymore." She shrugged. "It's too late now."

"It's not that far," he said, more to himself than her. He put the phone away and looked at her. "I take it this is personal and His and Her Majesties are opposed to this visit?"

"Yes, it's personal. I didn't tell them I had plans to visit this property during the official trip," she confessed.

"May I ask why?"

"It's complicated." After a brief hesitation, she continued. "My financial independence is tied to a trust fund set up by my great-grandfather, which I can't access until I turn thirty or get married, whichever happens first. I'd like to have access now, but Uncle Geoffrey and Aunt Nicolette are unwilling to see the terms changed."

"If you can't have access to it, why do you want to see this property?"

A little smile came to her lips. "Well, when I was looking for a loophole to the trust fund, I found a little unknown statute called the Law of Reparation. If a property, with or without a house, has sat vacant for seventy-five years or longer, anyone in the royal family can take it and have it restored with funds from the National Restoration Fund. The Law of Reparation goes back to the fifteenth century, if you can believe that."

Mr. Sterling nodded. "It makes sense. It was probably set up after the civil war of 1326. By the early 1400s, a lot of land would have been empty and ready for the picking. It would be a good way to sidestep the trust fund. Do your uncle and aunt know about this law?"

Emma cut back her enthusiasm. "They don't know about the loophole, and I'd appreciate it if you could keep this between us." She had only told Charlotte. "Once I find out whether the property and the plan are viable or not, I'll talk to my uncle and aunt."

"Your secret is safe with me." He glanced at the phone again, then stood. "If we leave right now, I think we'll get there in time to make your appointment."

She frowned. "Did I hear you right? Are you offering to drive me there?" She followed after him as he walked to the door.

"Yes, ma'am, you heard me right. I'll drive you to Hillside Meadows. We're not leaving to Inverly until tomorrow morning, anyway. There's plenty of time."

Emma reached for his hand with both of hers and grabbed his fingers tightly. "Thank you. Thank you so much."

His eyes snapped to their joined hands, her fingers holding his, his skin warming hers. He looked up at her, and the moment stretched for a frozen second until she dropped her hand, breaking the contact between them.

He stepped away first, then cleared his throat. "You're welcome, Your Highness. I'll meet you back here in a few minutes."

After he left and she closed and locked the door, Emma shook her head and chastised herself. What had she done, touching his hand like that? They were not friends, and she would do well to keep that in mind. For some reason, he'd decided to help her, but that didn't make him her friend.

When he returned, she gathered her purse, and they took the service elevator to the basement garage, where the car was parked.

"Under normal protocol for official visits, I have an extra set of keys, in case I need to drive you, for whatever reason. I didn't talk to the others officers and drivers, but I did inform my superior at the palace. As we're not supposed to be traveling, I doubt they'll notice the car is gone."

He didn't argue about her sitting in the front and held the door open while she sat on the passenger seat.

He pressed the ignition to start the car and brought the onboard navigation system online. "Is this right?" he asked, scrolling through the map. "Looks like Hillside Meadows is a small hamlet."

"It's quite small and remote," she confirmed. "Part of the reason why it remains abandoned."

"I'm guessing access is not the best either."

"I wouldn't think so." She pulled up the map on her phone. "The satellite photos are a few years old, so it could have changed."

"Let's not get our hopes up until we get there." He released the parking brake and followed the exit sign out of the garage.

Emma held her hands on her lap. She couldn't help but feel hopeful for what she might find at Hillside Meadows.

Chapter Twelve

*R*yan glanced at the onboard map once more, making sure he was still on the right road. The closer they approached to Hillside Meadows, the rougher the access became.

After driving away from Meeds along the coast toward the northeast of the country, the rain had simmered down but hadn't stopped until they exited the motorway in Craigwells, the largest town close to Hillside Meadows. They took a national road that led to a string of small villages, and, after so many days of unrelenting rain, the effects could be seen in debris everywhere.

Princess Emma pointed out each place by name as they passed it, how many inhabitants it had, how old it was, or even something that caught her eye. The discomfort and unease simmered between them—how could it not after everything that had transpired?—but she kept the silence from getting too awkward and the conversation too personal, almost as if they were two people getting to know each other on a first date.

The thought took Ryan by surprise. In the confines of the car, with both of them wearing casual clothes and on a road trip that was not official business, a frisson of familiarity lay just under the surface, something he had no right to imagine.

His grip tightened on the wheel at the memory of her grabbing his hand. It was only an impulsive response to his offer, nothing more; but despite knowing it didn't mean anything, the feelings it had stirred remained too strong.

Ryan stopped as they came to a narrow stone bridge with three arches—a common design in the countryside, simple and serviceable. The hamlet of Hillside Meadows sat on the other side of a river, a sort of peninsula connected by a centennial bridge and a gravel road that looked to have seen better days. A fork separated the road into two, the east side to Hillside Meadows and the west to other hamlets farther up along the banks. From their position, no other sounds of nature were discernible above the rushing waters of the river, as if everything else were less important. It was ominous, and Ryan hoped it didn't carry a portent of something more.

"Well, that's got to be the fullest river I've ever seen," Princess Emma commented.

"And the oldest bridge in the kingdom," he added.

She laughed at that and then pulled out her phone. "I was going to check when it was built, but I don't have reception."

He grabbed his phone. "I don't either." He wouldn't worry about it yet, not until they made the return trip.

"I hope the land agent is still coming."

"We'll soon find out," he said.

Ryan crossed the bridge slowly and gritted his teeth when they arrived on the other side. Up close, the gravel road was in worse condition than he'd first glimpsed, with deep potholes flooded with rainwater. He drove carefully, too slowly almost, wishing they had an all-terrain vehicle instead of a luxury sedan. They'd be lucky to make it there and back without any problems.

"I'm sorry," Princess Emma said. "I had no idea it would be like this."

"It's not your fault," he assured her. "I think the heavy rains of the past few days have made it worse."

When he and Princess Emma arrived at the property twenty minutes later, the land agent was there, sitting behind the wheel of a red Range Rover, an older model from the seventies. Of course the man would be driving the right kind of automobile.

"I should have asked before," Ryan started, "but why is there a land agent when the property is abandoned?"

"The county proper holds the rights to sell, and they were curious about my inquiries. I figured I'd better agree to a guided tour." Before exiting the car, the princess donned her pair of aviators and pulled on the knit hat she'd worn this morning. She turned to him. "I forgot to mention I'm using an alias."

"That's a good idea," he told her.

She lifted an eyebrow in a half smile. "Did I finally do something you approve of?"

Before he could find an answer, she was out the door on her way to meet the agent, a definite spring in her walk. Ryan locked the car and followed after her, giving her some privacy to talk to the man.

The hamlet consisted of a few acres of land alongside a dirt road, a handful of abandoned cottages, and an ancient manor house in serious disrepair. Centennial trees dotted the area and formed a natural barrier that kept the place apart from the rest of the landscape. Ryan only knew what the princess's plans were in general, not any of the specifics, but he couldn't see why she'd want this hamlet, so far away from everything and with such bad access to get here. The name of the place was definitely grander than the place itself.

She walked with the land agent, and Ryan trailed behind them as they peeked into every cottage and the ground floor of the house. From the top of the hill, to the west of the region, the neighboring hamlets were visible through the autumnal foliage, places that were inhabited and had working farms. The primitive beauty of the area invoked a raw feeling, a return to the roots and a simplicity of life, and Ryan couldn't disregard the appeal despite the property's less than stellar condition. At the same time, he couldn't help but wonder why the people had abandoned the hamlet. What had happened here?

After the agent left, Princess Emma approached where Ryan stood by the car. "Do you mind if I take a few more minutes?" she asked. "I want to make sure I have all the pictures I need."

He shook his head. "I don't mind at all. Go ahead."

She thanked him and left, repeating the route she'd taken before but at a clipped pace.

He followed her more sedately this time.

"Thank you," she said when they returned, cheeks flushed from the walk.

"Will it do?"

"I think it might." She looked around as if taking everything in one more time.

"One step closer to independence. I hope it works out for you," he added in sincerity.

"Thank you." She regarded him for a moment. "What do you think of the place?"

"It doesn't matter what I think." He softened his posture into a relaxed stance, as he wouldn't want her to think he was annoyed.

"It doesn't, but I'm still curious."

It didn't surprise him that she was. "I can see the appeal."

"But?"

"Why do you assume there's a *but*?" he asked, not masking his amusement.

"You're too pragmatic to not see beyond the appeal."

She'd gauged him right. "But the access is a deal breaker," he said.

"Maybe the possibilities are worth the bad access."

He was enjoying their exchange too much. "Possibilities can't make up for reality."

"Dream a little, Mr. Sterling. Take the possibilities for what they are."

"What's that, Your Highness?"

"Dreams sprinkled with reality."

He smiled. "You're the opposite of pragmatic, aren't you?"

"Which is what?" she asked in turn.

"Idealistic." Most likely to the core.

"Given the chance, I'll dress up reality in dreams and ideals any time I can." She opened the passenger door and looked at him from over the rim of her sunglasses. "Let's get going, Mr. Sterling. I'm starving. See, I can be pragmatic when the need arises."

Ryan chuckled lightly. "There's something I heartily support, ma'am."

It started raining again as they made their way back to the main road, and Ryan was soon reminded of the access road's condition. He drove slowly over the loose gravel and eased away from the many potholes.

"Whatever price they're asking for the hamlet and house," he started, "they need to deduct fifty percent for the new owner to rebuild this road."

Princess Emma nodded, but she didn't say anything. She winced as the car leaned in a deeper rut, her right hand flying to the door handle, which she gripped tightly.

Next time he drove her somewhere, he'd make sure they had the right kind of vehicle for the road conditions. This was almost primitive.

At last, they neared the bridge. As much as Ryan wanted to accelerate and cross to the other side, he continued at the same pace until they came to it. But something didn't look right.

Princess Emma sat up straight. "Is it me, or did the river swell in the past two hours?"

He brought the car to a gentle stop in front of the bridge and let the engine idle for a moment. "No, it's not only you. I think you're right."

When they had crossed before, the water level had reached just under the arches, but now the arches were no longer visible, and the raging waters threatened to spill onto to the bridge's deck and the banks on each side.

"It's flooding," she said, her voice low.

It wasn't safe to cross. He wouldn't risk the princess's safety, nor his own. As Ryan went over their options in his mind, the middle of the bridge gave away with a rumbling sound. A spray of water and rocks surged for a moment, rising in their direction, and then the rest of the bridge collapsed with a loud crack, right before their eyes.

He threw the car in reverse and stomped on the pedal, tires spinning on the gravel road as he backed up at full speed. Princess Emma gasped.

"Hang on," he said, an arm slung over the back of her seat and his head turned to the rear window.

Ryan reversed the car for an interminable moment, away from the river and onto the gravel and roadside debris, until a popping sound made him stop. The alarm on the dashboard pinged and blinked, alerting him to a sudden change in tire pressure. He put the car into park, holding back a curse, then turned off the engine and exited.

At the back, what he found was worse than he suspected—not one, but two flat tires. He squatted to take a better look, already knowing the car was done for.

The passenger side door opened and closed, and Princess Emma approached, her hood pulled up to shield her face. "A flat tire, huh?"

"Two," he replied, then stood, already completely soaked from the unrelenting rain.

"Oh."

"I'm afraid so." Changing a tire would be useless since the car only carried one spare.

Yards away from them, the waters raged, most of the bridge now gone. He slipped his phone out of his pocket and unlocked the screen to find the service still down.

"Mine isn't working either." Her tone carried hints of apology and worry.

Ryan nodded. "We might be too far away from a tower and out of service, or the rain has knocked wires down. Come on; we can't stay here."

"I was waiting for you to say that." Her tone was not as resigned as he'd expected. "What's the plan?"

Ryan opened the glove compartment and rummaged through it. "We need to find anything that might be useful and easy to carry. Then we'll walk till we find help at the next hamlet or until we get cell reception, whichever comes first." That was all he could do to keep her safe, both of them safe, until they were able to return to the hotel in Meeds.

He reached over to pop the latch to the trunk and went around to flip it open, hoping to find the emergency backpack he'd stored there.

After a moment, Princess Emma rounded his view, arms crossed over her chest, her hair partially hiding her face. "I'm sorry," she said. "This is my fault."

Ryan straightened and looked at her. "What do you mean? Of course it isn't." He understood why she'd think it was, but in truth, they were victims of unfortunate circumstances. The backpack lay where it was supposed to be, much to his relief, next to a small shovel and a reflective warning triangle. He unzipped the bag to check the contents.

"If I hadn't insisted on visiting, we wouldn't be stranded in the middle of nowhere."

"You're not taking into consideration all the other factors," he argued. "The weather, the road conditions, the bridge collapse. You can't control any of those." He meant the words, but a niggle of doubt couldn't be held back for giving in to her insistence. Too late for regrets.

The backpack contained two water bottles, several energy bars, a flashlight and batteries, a rolled-up blanket, a road flare, a small tool kit, and a first-aid kit. He hadn't planned to be in a remote location like this one, but once he returned to the palace, he would add a solar battery charger, toiletries, and even a sleeping bag, among other items. Protecting the princess was turning out to be more of an adventure than he'd anticipated.

After a second pass through the items, Ryan zipped up the backpack and closed the trunk. "It's not your fault," he repeated, then stepped away, all too aware of her nearness. Frustration flashed through him—of all the times to be thinking of how close they stood. How could he even think of that at a time like this?

She didn't look too convinced but didn't argue further.

They had to get away from the area as soon as possible, before anything else was swept away.

"Would you please help me get the car to the side?"

"Sure. What do you need?"

He had Princess Emma sit behind the wheel and put the gear in neutral while he pushed the car to the shoulder of the road.

After, he came around to the driver's side and held the door for her. "Do you have all your belongings?"

"Let me get my purse." She reached in the back seat and pulled it out, then slipped it on her shoulders. It was a small one, more stylish than useful.

Ryan put his backpack on. "When you were touring with the land agent, I noticed there's a hamlet to the west of here. I couldn't make out how large it is through the trees and hills, but I don't think it'll take us more than a few hours to walk there. It doesn't look to be any farther than ten to twelve miles away. We can make it."

She watched him for a moment, her expression placid, too neutral for him to guess what she was thinking or feeling. Was she worried about their circumstances, nervous about the isolation and the lack of phone service? "I know this is not an ideal situation, but I'm confident we can find help."

"Are you trying to ease my fears, Mr. Sterling? If you are, you can rest assured I'm not worried." She shrugged. "It's inconvenient, yes, and I still feel responsible for our situation, but I'm more worried about how my family is going to react when we don't make it back by tonight."

That had crossed his mind already.

If they didn't return, and couldn't get a message out in time, it would reflect badly on his record and his career as a protection officer. He was responsible for Princess Emma, and being stranded in the middle of nowhere without a vehicle would be heavily frowned upon, if not much worse.

But he would deal with that later.

Chapter Thirteen

*E*mma couldn't remember the last time she'd walked this long. She'd thought herself in good physical condition, but doing Pilates and cardio a few times a week was not the same as walking on the side of a country road without smooth sidewalks. The lack of proper shoes didn't help either. But she pressed on as if she were fine and not wanting to sit and rest like she'd never wanted anything more in her life. At least this road was paved, even though it could use a new topcoat. When she returned to the palace, she'd find out why this part of the kingdom showed such neglect.

Mr. Sterling walked beside her, on the outside. Was that some sort of gentleman behavior or the protocol of a protection officer? Maybe both.

Daylight faded faster out here than in the city. Amid the hills and trees, without buildings and traffic and streetlights every few feet, they would have been in near darkness if not for the flashlight he carried.

She glanced at his feet. He'd adjusted his pace to her slower one again. When they'd started out, she'd made sure to keep up with his stride, even though she suspected he could walk much faster if she weren't there. Almost three hours later, she was tired and hungry and cold, and there was no sign of the next hamlet. At least it had stopped raining. She was also thirsty, but wouldn't take another drink so soon—relieving herself in the woods was out of the question. Somehow, she knew Mr. Sterling wouldn't let her go more than a few yards away from him, and she wouldn't subject herself to that kind of embarrassment. Not yet; she wasn't that desperate.

The river ran among the trees and parallel to the road, its raging waters sounding almost as fierce from here as they had by the bridge. Even with the noise of birds and insects, and the rustling of tree leaves in the evening breeze, she could still make out the way their shoes scraped against the gravel shoulder. She'd run out of conversation topics with Mr. Sterling, and he'd stopped prodding her some time back.

He kept the stream of light pointed directly at her feet. How he didn't trip, she didn't know. She'd stumbled once already and would have fallen on the ground if not for him grabbing her by the elbow.

"Hold on, please." His voice interrupted her thoughts. "Could you hold the flashlight for a moment?"

Emma stopped and reached for the flashlight, then pointed it at what he was doing.

He unzipped his backpack and offered her an energy bar. "Here."

"Isn't that the last one?" she asked.

"It's for you."

That didn't answer her question. "I'm okay for now, thank you." She wasn't, not completely. Her feet hurt.

"Will you at least take the blanket?"

He didn't wait for her reply but draped it over her shoulders.

"Thank you." She resumed walking, still holding the flashlight with one hand and keeping the blanket in place with the other.

"You should take the energy bar. You need to keep up your strength," he insisted, catching up to her.

"And you don't?"

"I'm used to this," he replied matter-of-factly.

Emma rolled her eyes. "Really? How many times have you walked on a deserted country road in the dark?"

"I have more training than you."

He did, of course. "Why don't you admit to being condescending because I'm a woman?" She couldn't hide the irritation in her tone. "Or is it because I'm a princess? Which one is it?"

"Your gender and status have nothing to do with this."

"Sure," she huffed.

After a long minute, he said "I'm sorry."

Emma stopped and pointed the flashlight up between them to see his face. "Why are you apologizing? We both know it's my fault we're in this predicament. I was the one who made the appointment to come to Hillside Meadows, and you wouldn't have offered to drive me if I hadn't tried to come by myself."

When he didn't say anything to that, she resumed walking.

"Well, when you put it that way," he said at last.

Emma cut him a side glance, even though she couldn't see much of him. "You don't have to agree so readily. A gentleman wouldn't."

"I've already told you it's not your fault, but you're obviously intent on hearing the opposite from me." Despite his words, he kept his voice even. "Besides, I'm not a gentleman," he quickly added. "Only your protection officer, ma'am."

"As if you'd let me forget that," she huffed again.

"What does that mean?"

She stopped to look at him again. "It means—"

A loud rustling broke through the forest sounds. "What's that?"

Mr. Sterling brought a finger to his lips, and they listened intently as the grunts of an animal became more distinct.

"What kind of animal is it?" Emma asked. "Whatever it is, it's not that far."

He reached for his shoulder holster and drew out his gun. "I'm not sure. Most animals keep to higher altitudes and denser forests."

"Except for this one. Maybe the floods dislodged its burrow. What are we going to do?"

After another moment, he returned the gun to the holster. "Let's keep walking." He nudged her elbow.

"There's a wild animal stalking us and your plan of action is to keep walking? Are you not at all worried?" Emma tried to keep her voice calm, but the nerves were getting to her. Nerves and fear.

"Like you said, it's far enough. We'll worry if it gets closer."

"That's not what I said at all." She resumed walking next to him, closer than before. If he noticed, he didn't comment on it.

Her shoulders slumped. He didn't deserve her grumpy mood; it wasn't fair on her part. "I think I need to say—" Twin beams of light glinted in the distance from the opposite direction. "Is that a car?"

He turned to see. "The headlights of a car, yes."

The sound of an engine reached their ears, confirming the approach of a vehicle.

"Go ahead and wave the flashlight," he told her. "Stay behind me, and don't say anything. Let me do the talking."

As the vehicle turned around and came to a stop beside them, she scampered in front of Mr. Sterling who sighed most dejectedly while she approached the passenger door of an old pick-up truck. An older man wearing a newsboy cap greeted them from behind the wheel.

"Evening, folks," he said through the window, already rolled down halfway. "Are you in need of assistance?" He seemed to be in his late seventies and had the rugged look of someone who spent time outdoors, worn leather and deep grooves.

Emma stepped up to the window. "Good evening, sir. We could use a ride to the next village. Any chance you could drop us there?"

The man scratched the gray whiskers on his chin. "Well, no, it's quiet impossible. Sorry."

Emma's shoulders drooped. Did she dare ask him why? She was willing to breach good manners to find out.

Mr. Sterling bent over to talk through the window. "Do you know of a way for us to get to phone service?"

"I'm afraid not," the man replied. "Do you have a place to stay tonight?"

"We don't," Emma told him, her face inches away from the glass.

The man straightened his cap. "It's nothing fancy, but you're welcome to come home with me. My wife is the best cook in the county and Wednesday night is beef stew."

Emma smiled wide. "Oh, that would be so great, thank you."

She reached for the door handle, but Mr. Sterling stopped her and pulled her aside.

"What's the matter?" she asked him.

"We can't just get into some guy's truck," he said in a low voice.

She leveled him with a hard stare. "Maybe you don't mind spending the night outside, with your training and all, but I do."

She opened the truck door and slid inside. "Thank you so much, Mr.—"

"Baxter, Tom Baxter. You can call me Tom." He frowned at her. "You look a lot like—"

The light inside the truck was bright enough that he could probably see her features distinctly. "I get that a lot. You have no idea." She chuckled, hoping it sounded natural. "I'm Emily Summers." The lie slid out smoothly, as if she told it every day.

Tom looked behind her. "And you are?"

Mr. Sterling folded his big frame and sat beside her. "I'm Ryan, her husband." He casually dropped an arm on her shoulders, his other hand greeting the old man.

For some reason she couldn't fathom, Emma's jaw didn't slack, her eyes didn't widen. She relaxed her expression into a quasi-smile, cementing the bald-faced lie her protection officer had slipped in so easily, she was half-way to believing it herself.

What a pair of impostors they'd become.

"Thank you so much for the ride, sir," Mr. Sterling said.

"You're sure welcome." Tom shifted gears and pulled out. "Newlyweds?" he asked.

"How did you know?" Mr. Sterling tightened his hold on her, a wide smile on his face.

Tom smirked. "You just have that look about you."

Emma's right side and Ryan Sterling's left were pressed against each other—from shoulder to hip to thighs, his warmth radiating into her body. The contact heightened her awareness of him, and she could hardly concentrate on anything else.

Why had he introduced himself as her husband? He couldn't have said he was her protection officer, of course, but what about something else, anything that wouldn't put them so close? Maybe that was his plan— as a married couple, nobody would find it strange for them to be together all the time, especially as newlyweds. And she well knew how he wanted to keep an eye on her at all times.

A few minutes later, Tom took a right turn into a long gravel drive that led them to the front of a small brick house. The front door opened and a pair of black-and-white border collies bounded toward their owner with happy barks and wagging tails. They came around sniffing curiously as Emma and Mr. Sterling stood on the walk, and she gave them her hand to smell, then patted them on their heads.

"These two are Brutus and Nero. Come on, let's go inside, you bounders," Tom said to the dogs.

Emma and Mr. Sterling followed right behind. Inside, none of the light fixtures and lamps were on, but the house felt cozy and bright enough. Before anyone paid attention, she moved the ring she wore on the middle finger on her right hand to the ring finger on the left hand. It was a simple one, but she could say she didn't want to wear her nice band while traveling. She'd have to tell Mr. Sterling to say his was being resized.

"Hello, who do we have here?" At the end of the hallway, a woman approached with a smile, wiping her hands on her apron.

"These two youngsters are Ryan and Emily Summers." He turned to them and gestured to the woman. "This lovely lass is Mrs. Baxter, my Mary."

Mr. Sterling extended his hand. "Call me Ryan, please." When he turned to Emma, he mouthed *You too* to her. She glanced at him with a raised eyebrow. When had he turned so irritating? Of course she had figured out already that she needed to call him by his first name.

And he'd have to call her Emily.

"Come in, come in. Excuse our lack of lighting. The electricity went out the day before yesterday and hasn't been restored yet, but come get warm by the fire." She ushered them into the room closest to the front door. "I know it's only September, but it feels nice to have in the evenings."

A few large flashlights and portable oil lamps had been strategically placed toward the back of the room to offer illumination, while at the front, most of the light came from the fire.

"Thank you, Mrs. Baxter," Emma said, already extending her hands toward the grate. "I'm Emily, by the way."

"Call me Mary, dear." The lady straightened and watched Emma attentively. "Emily," she said at last. "Very pleased to meet you, Emily."

Had Mrs. Baxter recognized her? If she had, she didn't say anything about it, and Emma felt a pang of guilt for lying to these generous people.

Emma looked around. The room was comfortable and well lived in, with a large window to the front and a pair of couches flanking the fireplace. Next to the door that opened to the hallway sat a secretary desk and a loaded bookcase filled with books, with a chair, worn and beckoning. Through a wide arch, the back of the room led to a compact dining room, with a simple rectangular table, four chairs, and a sideboard with a display of traditional blue-and-white dishware. The kitchen was probably next, at the very back of the house.

Tom sat down by the fire and took off his boots. "I picked them up on the side of the road. They're newlyweds." The dogs settled on a rug by his feet.

"How lovely," Mary said. She grabbed her husband's boots and took them to the hallway. When she returned, she asked, "How long have you been married?"

"One month," Emma replied at the same time Ryan said, "One week."

They regarded each other for a moment, and Ryan winked at her. "A month already? Time flies when you're happy." He came closer to Emma, and his arm came around her shoulders again. "I hadn't noticed it's been that long, sweetheart."

He was good, she'd give him that. Even she was almost convinced of his sincerity. But it was only pretend.

So why did his arm around her have to feel so right? And the little term of endearment that warmed her heart?

The Baxters looked at the both of them, and Emma couldn't begin to guess what they thought of the pair of them. Some newlyweds they were, who couldn't get their dates straight.

"You better not forget her birthday," Tom said.

The four of them chuckled at the light remark.

"The stew is ready," Mary said. "Why don't you wash up? The powder room is off to the other side of the hallway."

The Baxters went on ahead to the kitchen. Once in the hallway, Ryan leaned Emma's way. "January sixteenth," he said in her ear.

Emma's skin raised in goosebumps, and she turned to find him with an earnest look in his eyes, already set on her.

"Did I get it right?" he whispered. "Your birthday?"

She nodded, not trusting her voice. Her awareness of him ramped up again—his masculine scent, his breath fanning her skin, and his low, deep voice ingraining in her every nerve. Her cheeks flamed, and she looked away. She had to put some distance between them and get a grip.

Of course he remembered her birthday—he knew facts about her, things he'd read on some file with her name on it. She'd do well not to be impressed. It was part of his job, after all.

That was all he knew, facts and numbers. Nothing more.

But it wasn't fair she didn't know his birthday.

Chapter Fourteen

*R*yan stood and pulled out a chair for Emma when she joined him and the Baxters at the table. She looked less flushed than before and had removed the sweater and the blanket he'd given her earlier. The house was warm, and he hoped she was finally comfortable. Even though she hadn't complained once during their walk after the bridge collapsed, Ryan had seen her expression when she thought he wasn't looking. At least for tonight they had a place to stay, thanks to the Baxters' kindness. He tried to catch her eye, but she wouldn't look at him. Was she mad he'd introduced them as newlyweds? Or for the way he'd draped his arm over her shoulders several times already? Or maybe both. An explanation was due, if she agreed to listen to him.

Mary ladled a hearty portion of stew into a wide bowl and handed it to Emma. "It's a simple dinner, but it's home cooked and home baked." She cut a thick slice of bread and gestured for Emma to take a piece.

"Thank you, Mary." Emma took a bite and closed her eyes. "It's so good," she said, with a look of complete joy and contentment, as if it were the best thing she'd ever eaten.

Ryan smiled at her, and she curbed her easy expression. They definitely needed to talk.

If he had one word for the meal he and Princess Emma shared with the Baxters it would be *comfortable*. He liked the unhurried, unpretentious way it was, just four people around a simple table sharing a simple, delicious meal.

"Now tell me why I found you two on the side of the road today," Tom said, then sat back in his chair.

Ryan turned to Emma, and she nodded at him. "We went to Hillside Meadows and on the way back the bridge collapsed," he said.

Mary covered her mouth, and Tom's eyes widened. "How did you escape that?" he asked.

"We noticed the river looked full when we crossed," Emma said. "But when we returned, it looked worse."

"The bridge fell before we got on it, thankfully," Ryan said. "I put the car in reverse right away, and the back tires popped on something in the gravel. We only had one spare, so we left the car behind to find help."

"You're lucky you escaped with only two blown tires," Tom said gravely.

Ryan nodded. It had been close. He hadn't said anything to Princess Emma to spare her the worry, but she was an intelligent woman and didn't miss much.

"We couldn't find cell service, which means we weren't able to call for help," Princess Emma said.

Ryan turned to Mary. "You said you've been without power for two days. What about phone service?"

The old lady shook her head. "I'm sorry, dear. No power and no phone. Not since the storms."

"And the road to Blackwigg is flooded," Tom added. "That's why I couldn't take you there."

"So we're effectively isolated," Ryan said.

Mary nodded. "For a coupla days, dear. If it doesn't rain more."

"The road runs parallel to the river," Tom said. "When the waters go down, the road will clear. Then I'll take you there. Not a day sooner."

"You're welcome to stay with us for the duration, of course," Mary offered. "The house is small, but we have everything we need and we can certainly make room for you."

"You're so generous and kind, Mary. You too, Tom. Thank you so much," Princess Emma said. "We're really grateful, aren't we, Ryan?"

It caught him by surprise, the way she said his first name as naturally as if she'd been saying it forever. He watched her, kept his gaze on her, until he remembered the others expected a reply from him.

"Yes, we are, ma'am—macita. Mamacita," he quickly corrected. For good measure, he leaned toward her and placed his arm around her for a side hug. "Mi mamacita," he added with a small smile. If he could slap himself, he would. First for the slip up immediately after she'd said his name, then for the very lame coverup.

The Baxters stared at him, probably wondering what was going on.

"It's an endearment," Princess Emma said. She touched his hand, and he almost jumped at the contact. "In Spanish."

At least she came to his rescue instead of leaving him to explain that one. One more thing he had to apologize for when they had a moment alone.

"Oh, that's cute," Mary said after a moment that bordered on awkward. "There's a small bedroom in the loft. It hasn't been used in some time, but we can make the bed with fresh linen. I think it'll be warm enough. The chimney wall runs up there."

"I'm sure they can keep each other warm, dear," Tom said with a wink and a light chuckle.

Emma's cheeks pinked, and she looked away. They were expected to sleep in the same bed. What had he done? He'd obviously not considered this when he so breezily introduced himself to Tom as her husband, with the sole intent to stay close to her. He chanced a glance at her but she didn't look at him. They'd have to pretend sharing a bed was perfectly normal.

But of course he wouldn't get in the bed with her. The floor would have to do. It wouldn't be the first time he'd slept on the floor while on a job. There was no other solution. Sharing a bed with the princess was out of the question.

After they helped the Baxters clear the table and wash the dishes, Mary took Emma to find linens and make the bed in the loft. Not wishing to crowd them, Ryan stayed behind with Tom.

"Just a little suggestion," Tom started. "Make sure your new bride is doing okay with everything that happened today. Have a talk with her."

Ryan nodded. "I will."

"Sometimes wives get this idea they need to keep things inside so as not to worry us." Tom shrugged. "But it's not good for them, or us."

"She might be worried about her family when they find out we didn't return to Meeds tonight. They're expecting her—us—back home tomorrow. And we can't get the word out." Emma was not his wife, but he would have a talk with her and find out how she was feeling about their situation. If their absence hadn't been noticed by now, it certainly would by morning. It frustrated him that he couldn't be more proactive about it, but there was literally nothing that could be done.

"Well, you know how women are," Tom said with an air of finality, as if what he'd just said was part of a secret code between married men.

Ryan pretended he knew as well, when he really didn't have a clue.

He and Tom stayed at the dining table and talked about the farm and the hamlet of Blackwigg for some time until Mary popped in from the hallway.

"I'm off to bed. I left towels upstairs, and the bedroom is ready. The shower is next to the kitchen, and I'm sure Emily will tell you the rest. Good night, Ryan."

"Good night, Mary," he said. "Thank you for the hospitality."

Tom stood and handed the oil lamp to Ryan. "I'm going to bank the fire and go to bed too. Have a good night."

"Thank you, Tom, for everything."

After Tom was done, he shuffled away. The house grew silent and the shadows long, cast by the small lamp on the table. Ryan sat there for a moment, cataloging today's failures—his failures. Princess Emma was supposed to be at the hotel in Meeds, they both were, so they could leave to Inverly in the morning for the last day of visits before returning to the palace. Not stuck in the middle of nowhere without a way to move forward or contact anyone.

For someone who was so intent on doing the best he could to advance in his career, he sure knew how to mess up.

Ryan grabbed his backpack from where he'd left it and took the lamp with him to the small bathroom, where he changed his shirt and washed up the best he could. He'd have to sleep in his undershirt and jeans. He put it off a few minutes longer, then finally climbed the stairs. At the top, he knocked softly at the door, leaning in to listen for any sounds from the bedroom. Had Emma gone to bed already?

"Come in," she said quietly from inside.

He hesitated for a second before turning the knob and pushing the door open. Immediately in front of the door sat a wrought iron bed, one of the antique black ones with curlicues, dressed in a colorful bedspread.

Emma sat to one side, under the sheets, with her legs crossed and her back slightly leaning forward, away from the pillows. From what he could see, she wore some kind of long, loose nightshirt. Or maybe it was one of Mary's nightgowns. With her dark long hair in a braid over her shoulder, she was a vision of loveliness. He swallowed past the lump in his throat.

Ryan went in and closed the door behind him, then set the oil lamp on top of the chest of drawers and hung his sweatshirt on the peg nearby. Like Mary had said, the headboard was flush against the chimney wall. Other than the chest, the bed, and a small nightstand, the bedroom was void of any other furnishings. A woven rug covered the plank floor by the bed, and a dormer-style window with white curtains was tucked under the lower pitch of the roof to his right. He'd stay away from that side, as he wouldn't fit standing. Everything was small. Was there even enough room for him to sleep on the floor?

"I won't bite, Mr. Sterling," Emma said, bringing back his attention to her.

"Ryan," he corrected. "Call me Ryan, please. We can't keep protocol and titles while we're here."

"I have no problem calling you Ryan as long as you call me Emily."

"Right," he agreed. "Emily." It wasn't her name, and the word felt all wrong. He'd just have to get used to addressing her without the title and by a name that wasn't hers.

"What happened to your gun and holster?" she asked.

He tipped his chin toward the backpack. "I managed to slip them off and stuff them in there when we came in."

He took two steps and sat on the mattress on the opposite side of the bed, leaning down to untie his shoes.

The springs squeaked loudly, and his body went completely still.

For a moment, everything stopped and silence reigned.

"It gets worse," Emma—Emily—said. She scooted to the edge of the mattress on her side, the bed squeaking along with her the whole way.

"For real?"

"At least their bedroom is on the other side of the house and not directly below," she said, a hint of humor in her voice.

"If they hear all the squeaking, they're going to think—" he cut himself short from saying the rest.

"They'll think we took Tom's suggestion," she finished for him.

Was she teasing? He glanced at her and caught the pull of a smile before she turned to the window.

He reached down to his shoes again, releasing another set of squeaks.

On second thought, he'd keep his shoes on.

Moving carefully, Ryan sat sideways and faced her. "I'd like to apologize to you for the situation."

She frowned. "The situation?"

"It wasn't my intention to impose myself on you, and I'm sorry for that."

"You mean sharing a bedroom and a bed? Of course it was your intention." She took a deep breath. "I know why you did it. You wanted to ensure you stayed close to me, and what better way than to tell people we're newlyweds? The perfect cover. Only you failed to think it through all the way to this. Admit it."

"Yes. I mean, no. I didn't think it through at first. And yes, I did want to stay close to you. You're still my principal, ma'am." He shook his head. "Emma. I mean, Emily," he corrected himself once more. "Sorry, the names are kind of close."

She nodded. "Just call me Em. That way you can't mess it up."

He looked at her. "Just Em? Are you sure?"

"Yes, it's fine."

It was a nickname and it implied a closeness between them they didn't have in their relationship, but it was the kind of intimacy expected between a couple. Besides, it would solve the problem of him mixing up the names.

"Does anybody else call you that?"

"My brother and my cousins sometimes."

Her family called her Em, and she'd asked him to call her the same. Why did his heart jump at the implication? There was none. He wasn't part of her family and never would be. They weren't even friends.

"Em," he said in a low tone, holding her gaze. This time, it felt right.

Her eyes widened a fraction with some fleeting emotion he couldn't decipher. He expected her to look away, but she didn't, and the moment spun into a subtle thread of connection between them, the kind he'd remember for a little while.

He cleared his throat, effectively cutting the tie. "Tomorrow I'll hike to the highest point in the area to see if I can get any cell service."

"Can I come?"

"I'll go faster by myself."

She frowned. "You're no fun."

He couldn't tell if she was serious or not. "I'm sorry but—"

She held a hand up. "I understand. You don't have to explain."

He continued. "I also want to check the road where it's flooded and see how bad it really is. If there's any way I can cross to Blackwigg and get hold of a phone, I need to try."

"Are you really that concerned?"

"Your family will be worried for you. Nobody knows where we are or what happened to us."

"That's true." Her shoulders drooped. "I hope they won't be thinking the worst."

"I'm afraid it's a possibility," he agreed. "The car has a tracker, but I don't know if they'll be able to ping it. Same with our phones without service. Even if we can't leave for a couple of days, contacting the palace is imperative." He couldn't let Chief Officer Peters and everyone else think they'd been in an accident, or worse, that he'd let the princess get abducted. Unpardonable.

She nodded. "And in the meantime?"

"In the meantime, we continue with our cover as Ryan and Emily Summers, stranded newlywed couple."

"That's it?" she asked.

"The simpler we keep it, the easier it'll be to not make mistakes."

"I hate lying to the Baxters. They've been so kind to us."

"Don't think of it as lying. It's about keeping them safe. The less they know, the better it is for everyone involved."

She cocked her head to the side, as if considering him from a new angle. "Is that what you tell yourself?"

"It's the way it is. It may not always be pretty or polite, but if it keeps people safe, then it's good."

He reached for the pillow closest to him, and she visibly startled. Did she really think he'd use the bed and lie next to her? As jumpy as she was, the thought clearly repulsed her.

"I'll sleep on the floor." He grabbed the pillow and stood, took the two steps to the chest of drawers, and doused the oil lamp.

"Do you even have room to stretch out?" she asked.

"There's enough."

The other lamp glowed softly from her side of the bed, and he waited for her to extinguish it.

"Here. At least take this." She stood and grabbed a bundle he'd failed to notice, and when she walked in his direction, the light from behind her filtered through the thin material of the nightgown and revealed all her contours.

She padded in his direction, and Ryan swallowed, his chest tight, unable to keep his eyes away from her.

By the time reason returned to him, he'd seen more than he had any right to. He cast his eyes down and took the quilt from her, keeping himself carefully contained so as to not touch her in any way. "Thank you."

"You're welcome," she said.

Ryan put the pillow on the floor, lay down on the rug, and spread the quilt on top. Emma returned to bed, the springs protesting loudly until she stopped moving. After a moment, the squeaks came again, and then the bedroom plunged in darkness and silence.

"First thing tomorrow, I'm oiling those bed springs," he said.

She chuckled lightly. "I heartily agree with that."

"Are you okay?" he asked.

"Why wouldn't I be? We have a dry, warm place to stay and had a good dinner. Not to mention the excellent company. Couldn't ask for more tonight."

Was he the excellent company, or did she mean the Baxters?

Her reply surprised him. "I wouldn't have expected that a princess would be so easily satisfied," he confessed.

"I never asked to be a princess. I don't despise it, and I know there are perks, but it's not something I ever had a choice in, and I'd love to try *not* being one. That's part of the reason why I went to Hillside Meadows," she said, after a pause.

Her tone was confidential, almost intimate, and he waited for more. Was it the darkness in the room that prompted her to share something personal?

"You might think there isn't much there," she continued, "but to me it's full of possibilities, like being an ordinary person, and waking up in the morning with the day before me without obligations to fulfill and the expectations of so many people."

"Everyone has obligations. If I want a paycheck, I'm obligated to work," he said.

The springs squeaked as she moved on the bed. Was she getting closer? He tensed in anticipation.

"That's true," her voice came from the edge of the mattress, her breath fanning the top of his hair.

If he reached up his fingers, he'd be able to touch her face.

She continued, unaware of how much he was enjoying her admissions.

"But you were able to choose the career you wanted. Mine was thrown upon me at birth, and, sometimes, I just wish for a simpler life." She settled back down.

"Like what the Baxters have here."

"Yes, something like what they have. Simple and free." After a moment, she added, "I'm sorry. It sounds like I'm complaining, and that's far from the truth. I am okay."

He hesitated before asking the next question. "And do you feel safe?"

She replied after a longer pause, her voice already heavy with sleep. "I'm always safe with you."

Chapter Fifteen

*E*mma woke with the terrible sound of a battering ram against her door. A whack, then something falling, clattering. Only it wasn't on her door—it was somewhere outside the house.

She rolled over to the other side and found the hazy morning light seeping through lacy curtains on a mansard window. The Baxters' attic.

Her memories of the day before came rushing—the drive to Hillside Meadows, the bridge collapse, walking on a deserted road, and getting a ride from Tom Baxter. Thanks to Tom and Mary Baxter, she and Ryan had been fed a delicious dinner and had been given a place to sleep.

Ryan Sterling.

She peeked over the other side of the bed, but there was no one on the floor. The pillow and quilt lay folded at the foot of the bed, and he was gone. What time was it, anyway, and where was he?

Emma walked to the window and drew the curtains aside only to be met with a gossamer layer of gray. Visibility was low, hiding the front yard and the road beyond, and the humidity dripped on both sides of the windowpane. She shivered.

After changing and making the bed, she walked downstairs and found Mary in the small kitchen. "Good morning."

Mary turned from the old gas stove. "Good morning, Emily. Did you sleep well?"

"Very well, thank you. I think I overslept. What time is it?" Emma's phone battery had died and she couldn't tell how late in the morning it was with the foggy weather.

"Just a little after nine." Mary gestured at a round clock on the wall. "I'm glad you slept well. I was afraid the bed upstairs would be too small for you and Ryan, but looks like you made it work."

Emma glanced at the clock. "I don't usually sleep this late. I'm sorry."

"Don't apologize, dear. You're on your honeymoon. Enjoy it while you can. How do you like your coffee?"

"Milk and one sugar, please. Thank you, Mary."

Mary put a sturdy cup on the table and gestured at the sugar pot. "I'm afraid we're out of milk, but we do have powdered creamer."

Emma leaned against the counter. She stirred one spoonful of sugar in her cup, then added creamer and stirred again. "This is wonderful, thank you. Have you seen Ryan? He didn't wake me up when he left."

"Isn't that the sweetest husband, he let you sleep in. All Tom wanted to do on our honeymoon was—" Mary cleared her throat. "Anyway, yes, I saw your husband this morning. He asked to borrow a flashlight and a pair of sturdy boots and took to the hills."

Emma sipped her coffee. "Do you know if he was able to find a cell signal?"

"I don't think so, dear. He came back an hour later, had some coffee and eggs, and then offered to split the woodpile." Mary placed a plate with two pieces of toast on the table. "Would you like some eggs as well?"

"You didn't have to make me breakfast, Mary, but thank you. This toast looks great." Emma buttered one piece, then the other. "What do you mean by splitting the woodpile?"

Mary smile in a conspiratorial fashion. "Well, dear, let me show you. Bring your cup with you." She grabbed the plate with toast and left the kitchen. Emma followed, curious to see what the old lady was talking about.

They walked to the front room. Mary set the plate on a little table by the window and drew the curtains aside. Then she stood to the right and pointed outside to the left.

"Right over there."

A shed of some sort with a sloping roof sat perpendicular to the house, a stack of cut wood to the left and Ryan in the center, just off the overhang. He swung an ax in the air and brought it down on a log, its sides splitting and falling to the ground. Right away, he picked another log and repeated the action. This was what she'd heard in the loft bedroom.

Emma stared at the view, at the show of force that emanated from him so naturally, her eyes wide and her cup midway to her mouth. He wore a sleeveless tank that showed his physique to great advantage, and his skin glistened, part sweat and part humidity, mixed so well she couldn't tell where one started and the other ended.

Wasn't he cold? It wasn't raining, but the sun wasn't warm enough to burn the clinging fog just yet.

Intellectually, she knew he had to be in great condition for his job, and imagined he probably went to a gym and worked out every day, but seeing him like this, with that level of concentration, was different. This was a task that resulted in a tangible product, cut firewood for the Baxters. Pretty sure they were set through the winter.

"Your husband makes splitting wood look like an Olympic sport," Mary said.

Emma bit her bottom lip to hide a grin. "He sure does." She kept watching Ryan. Mesmerized. There was no other word for it. "I didn't even know he could swing an ax like that." There was so much she didn't know about him. They'd been together every day all week and she didn't know much more now than she did on the day she met him in Aunt Nicolette's office.

But that wasn't true. She did know about him—he was loyal to her, he was always polite, dedicated to his job, and willing to do what had to be done. He was also observant and thoughtful, as he'd noticed when she was hungry and had brought her food; he was smart, as he'd figured out her plan to leave; and he was extremely patient, as evidenced during her shopping trips in Castlebridge, and yesterday, with her slower pace and her complaining.

"Apparently he hadn't done it before. Tom explained the mechanics of the job, and by the third swing, Ryan looked like he was a born lumberjohn."

Emma chuckled. "You mean a lumberjack." All he needed was a flannel shirt, but that sleeveless cotton undershirt looked much better on him than any plaid ever would. It left his wide shoulders and well-defined arms on a very attractive display. To think he was hiding all that under the suits he wore on a daily basis. What a shame.

157

"I think he split enough wood to last until spring," Mary said. "Let me go get another cup of coffee, and you can take it to him."

Before Emma had a chance to reply, Mary was gone to the kitchen. She returned promptly with another cup of creamy coffee, and she traded Emma's for the new one. "Take it to him and tell him we have enough wood." She threw a wool shawl over Emma's shoulders and opened the front door for her. "Off you go, dear."

Emma walked slowly, not sure how she'd get Ryan's attention but as she approached, he put down the ax and started stacking the wood in the shed. Of course he'd know she was there. Nothing ever escaped him.

"Hi," she said. "I've got some coffee for you."

"Hi." He reached over to a wood post and grabbed a flannel shirt and put it on, leaving it unbuttoned. The lumberjack look was complete after all. Emma's mouth quirked.

Even faded and missing some buttons, the shirt did nothing to hide Ryan's appeal.

He took the cup from her. "Thank you." After a long sip, he said, "I found it in the back."

"Found what?" she asked, not understanding what he meant.

"This plaid shirt. I found it at the back of the house, and Mary said I could use it. You were staring at it," he added.

He'd caught her looking, of course. "Just wondering."

The dogs came bounding from behind the house and stopped in front of her, tails wagging and grins wide.

Emma patted their heads. "Where have you guys been?" She hadn't seen them since last night.

"They followed me on my walk and went back to Tom when we returned," Ryan said.

She watched the dogs leave the way they'd come after they lost interest and turned to find Ryan looking at her.

"Did you sleep well?" He asked.

She nodded. Remarkably well, because he'd been in the same room, but of course, she wouldn't say that to him. "And you?"

"Well enough."

Not likely, on that old floorboard and without much space, despite what he'd said. Would he find her too forward if she invited him to share the bed tonight? He would be more comfortable, and it wasn't like anything else would happen.

She gestured to the ax and the woodpile. "Was this for exercise or for the sake of frustration?"

"Definitely both," he said, then took another sip.

"I take it you didn't find cell service."

He shook his head. "Nothing. This fog doesn't help much either. I'm not familiar with the area, so I don't know if there are higher spots, and I didn't have the time to go farther."

He didn't say it. He didn't have to—he wouldn't go farther because of her. As it was, it surprised her he'd left her with the Baxters. He must have been confident they were truly isolated and not at risk of anything imminently dangerous to her.

"Maybe it won't be so foggy tomorrow," she said.

"Let's hope." He tipped up the rest of the coffee and handed the cup back to her when she extended her hand for it.

"Thank you," he told her.

"You're welcome. Are you coming in?"

"I want to finish this first. It's the least I can do."

Somehow, she knew he was the kind of man who couldn't stand to feel useless. "Come in for a warm shower when you're done."

"Warm shower? Did the power come back on?"

"Not yet. They have some kind of gas-powered device. I had a warm shower last night, and it felt amazing."

He frowned lightly and held up a hand but let it drop. "But your hair wasn't wet."

"No, of course not." She grabbed the tail of her braid and brought it over shoulder. "It takes me over an hour to dry my hair with a good-quality hairdryer. I don't wash it every day."

He watched her hair for another moment, as if fascinated by it. Was he? Did he not have a girlfriend? Or maybe his girlfriend had short hair and washed it every day. Were protection officers allowed to date and have girlfriends?

The thought startled her. When they returned to the palace, she'd make some discreet inquiries. For the sake of curiosity, nothing more.

He stepped back from her. Somehow, in the last few moments, they'd gravitated closer to each other.

Emma clasped the shawl with her free hand. "I'll see you inside?"

"I'll be there soon."

She turned to leave but stopped when he called her name.

"Em?"

Ryan hesitated, then walked toward her. "Emma," he said in a lower tone, coming even closer. "There's something we didn't discuss last night."

This time, they stood near enough to touch, so close she could raise her hand and splay it on his chest, right over that undershirt he wore. She tightened her fingers around the mug instead.

"What's that?"

He raised his eyes to the house and then returned them to her. "If we're newlyweds, I think Tom and Mary will have some expectations about the way we treat each other in front of them." He pitched his voice even lower, like he was telling her a secret.

"They might," she answered, her gaze dipping to his mouth. What was he trying to tell her?

"I respect you too much to do anything against your will," he continued. "Unless you were in danger."

"Right," she agreed with a nod.

"How do you feel about public displays of affection?"

"Like yesterday, when you put your arm around me?" Was that what he meant?

"Something more like this." Slowly, he raised his hand until his fingers touched her chin, tipping her face up to him. She froze in place, and he dropped his hand; then he bent down, and his lips rested on the corner of her mouth in a faint touch.

Light, firm.

Almost perfect.

At the last minute, she had the presence of mind to close her eyes, narrowing all her attention to the exact spot where the thin, sensitive skin of her lips converged too close to his. But not close enough. Was it a kiss?

Her heart jumped in her chest at the outburst of feeling—so many feelings—and her blood rushed to her head.

Emma swayed when Ryan pulled back. His hands took her elbows, steadying her. She opened her eyes to find him watching her with an expression she couldn't decipher in those warm chocolate eyes.

"Mary was watching us from the window," he said.

Emma's eyes widened. Was that why he'd almost kissed her? Because Mary had been watching them?

"Was that okay?"

"Okay," was all she could muster with a nod.

Of course there was no other reason for that frustrating almost kiss. Ryan "Follow All The Rules" Sterling had to keep their cover intact. It was all for show.

He pressed an object into her hand. "Here, you dropped the mug. Good thing my foot broke its fall."

It wasn't the only thing that had dropped; only her heart couldn't be picked up as easily.

She mumbled a hasty goodbye and retreated to the house, anxious to put some distance between them.

When she approached the window, there was no one there.

Chapter Sixteen

*A*fter cutting and stacking wood, Ryan cleared the rest of the debris leftover from the rain storms in the Baxters' yard. He finished a morning of working outside by raking the gravel that led from the road to the front door. Between the lingering fog and the low-hanging clouds, the sun had barely made an appearance, and the air had a nip to it. Still, he had to keep busy and useful. With the power and phone lines still out, there was nothing else to do but wait.

He'd kept an eye on the front window, but hadn't seen Emma since she'd brought the cup of coffee to him. She wasn't the kind of woman who scared easily—he knew that much about her—but he couldn't blame her for keeping away from him.

Why had he kissed her? Not even a real one, just an off-to-the-side peck.

Mary had been at the window only briefly, most likely not long enough to even witness that wisp of a kiss. But he'd done it all the same.

As light as it was, it made an impression on him, one that he couldn't forget, playing in a loop at the front of his mind. Physical exertion as a distraction hadn't worked, and he could still feel the warmth of her skin on his cold lips—the tingling, the heat, the barrage of feelings he wasn't ready to deal with, some undefinable sense of near completion and belonging. He wanted to understand it but still couldn't, still held back.

Ryan crossed the yard and walked around the back to the other side of the house where the Baxters kept their truck in a detached garage.

Tom sat inside the vehicle listening to the radio, the engine running, the door on the driver's side wide open, and the hood raised. The dogs lay nearby, snoozing.

"Any news?" Ryan asked.

"Lots of flooding and power outages," Tom replied, turning the volume down. "Phone lines still down. Roads closed." He shrugged. "Nothing to do but wait."

"What about the weather forecast?"

"Another day or two of rain up north. Not here, but the rivers will keep swelling until the rain stops."

Ryan nodded. "Unfortunately, it will take a while for the flooding to go down even after the rain stops." He gestured to the hood. "Is there a problem there?"

Tom turned off the engine and joined Ryan by the front of the truck. "I was going to check the oil level and got distracted." He chuckled. "Old age."

Ryan looked around the space and found a stack of old newspapers. He ripped a page and folded it in half, then walked to the truck, removed the dipstick, wiped it, and repeated. "It's running kind of low, actually," he told Tom.

"I think I have a new quart of engine oil around here somewhere."

Ryan spent the next few minutes adding oil to the old truck while Tom told him stories, then he proceeded to clean the windows and wipe the dashboard.

At some point, Mary brought them cold meat-and-cheese sandwiches which Ryan and Tom ate in the garage. Ryan found things to do for the next hour, small tasks that required height or strength, or both, to save Tom some work and to alleviate the load, wishing there were more he could do for the couple.

"When I gave you and your wife a ride, I didn't intend to make you work for it," Tom said. "But I think you're like me when I was your age."

"Unable to stand still?" Ryan asked.

"You're not the kind to sit and wait, are you?" Tom asked.

"I'm not," Ryan agreed. "Give me something to do and put me to work."

"You did plenty today already. Leave some for tomorrow." Tom stood and walked out of the shed, the dogs following. "We're running out of light, anyways. Time to go in and see what our wives have been doing all day."

"You wouldn't happen to have any clothes that might fit me, would you?" Ryan asked. "I need a shower." Without the power restored, he wouldn't be able to use the washer.

Tom eyed Ryan and rubbed his chin. "I think I might."

The shower room was just off the kitchen, an addition attached to the main house at a later date, if Ryan guessed right. He caught a glimpse of Emma working on dinner beside Mary, both women talking animatedly and laughing. Their eyes connected for a moment, her mouth stretching in a small smile, and his own widened in response.

Maybe, just maybe, she wasn't mad at him for that ghost kiss he'd sneaked on her without warning.

He could only hope.

After his shower, Ryan dressed in borrowed clothes that were a bit short on him and entered the kitchen. The room was small and straight, without a place to sit down, but he found everyone congregated there, even the dogs, who lay near the door to the backyard.

"Ryan," Mary said. "Dinner is almost ready, and you must be hungry. You worked so hard today." She looked between him and Emma. "And you two didn't even spend any time together."

"No, we didn't," he said, crossing the few feet that separated him from Emma. He slipped an arm over her shoulders and drew her in a side hug, then dropped a quick kiss to her forehead, just below her hairline. She surprised him by wrapping an arm around his back and leaning into him before he let her go.

His heart revved. She fit much too well beside him and he liked her there, the feeling of her curves and warmth, that rogue sense of belonging with her.

They all carried the platters of food to the table, a hearty dish of noodles and vegetables, and sat down.

"This is delicious, Mary," he said. "Thank you." He hadn't realized how hungry he was until now.

"Emily made dinner," Mary said with a bright smile. "Your wife is a fast learner."

He turned to Emma. "Truly?" She could cook?

"I only followed Mary's recipe," Emma replied, cheeks pink.

"Don't sell yourself short," he said. "You did the work, and it's really good."

"Thank you," she said in a low voice.

"See, I told you he'd like it," Mary said to Emma, then turned to him. "She was concerned you wouldn't."

Ryan scrambled to say something that sounded plausible. "We haven't had a lot of chances to cook at home yet." Another lie.

"We're still getting used to each other's tastes," Emma said almost at the same time.

Mary's eyes lit with curiosity. "I remember those early days of newlywed life, discovering what we liked and didn't like. Of course, in those days, we didn't move in together until after the wedding."

"We didn't either," Ryan added quickly. It didn't matter if his and Emma's marriage was fake and non-existent—he wouldn't let the Baxters' imaginations run wild. He reached for Emma's hand and gave it a squeeze. "We're more comfortable with being traditional."

Emma blushed again, then nodded and returned the gesture. "We are."

"Nothing wrong with that," Mary said. "You have plenty of time to discover each other."

They didn't really, not in any measure, but oh, how much he wanted to.

"How long have you been married?" Emma asked Mary.

He'd just been about to ask something similar, with the intent of deflecting the conversation away from them, and was glad to see Emma had the same idea.

For the rest of dinner, Mary and Tom shared stories of their early days as a couple, amusing Ryan and Emma with their colorful tales of adjusting to married life. Afterward, he insisted on clearing up the table, but Emma and Mary kicked him out of the kitchen under the pretense of getting dessert ready.

On the sofas by the fire, they ate a warm bread pudding drizzled in caramel, he and Emma sitting opposite the Baxters. Mary excused herself early, and Tom watched her go with a hesitant look.

"I'll bank the fire, Tom," Ryan offered.

"Much obliged," Tom said, then stood from the sofa. "In that case, I shall follow my wife. Good night, Mr. and Mrs. Summers."

"Have a good night," Ryan said.

After Tom left, Ryan and Emma remained on the sofa, the fire waning in the grate. He braced himself for her to move away from him, anticipating the way he'd miss her, but she didn't, and he relaxed again.

"They're a cute couple," Emma said.

"Yes, they are. A little too curious at times."

"Almost inappropriate," she added with a chuckle.

Ryan joined her. "Definitely inappropriate."

"Some older people think they've earned the right to ask everything, like Mary."

He nodded, still amused. "Or say anything at all, like Tom."

After a quiet moment, she said, "Sometimes, I wonder if my parents would have grown to be like that in their older years."

He'd read her file and knew her personal history, how her parents had died in an accident when she was only eight. "What were they like?"

"I don't remember situations, but I do remember how they liked to have fun with me and my brother. Oliver has more memories than I do since he was older when it happened."

"I'm sorry. It must be hard."

He felt her nod against him. "As young as I was, I still miss them, more so around the holidays and special occasions. But I never felt like I'd lost everything. Uncle Geoffrey and Aunt Nicolette were there for me and Oliver every day, and my cousins as well, like we were still that big family, like my parents were only on an extended trip until we could be reunited."

"And now that all of you are grown up, are you still close?"

"We are, even though it's harder now. For the longest time, the six of us kids did everything together. Alex, Stefan, and Henry found love and got married first, then Oliver and Charlotte did too, and here I am, the last single one, trying to find my independence and a cause to contribute to, while being true to myself and loyal to my family. No pressure." She chuckled nervously.

"Are you sure you're not the one putting the pressure on yourself? From the little I know of your family, they don't seem to be the kind to push you against your will."

Her eyebrows pulled in concentration, and she hesitated.

He'd gone too far with his observations. "I said too much. I'm sorry. I shouldn't—"

"No, you're right," she interrupted. "They don't push me into anything I don't want, but sometimes they still see me as the baby and are a bit overprotective. I also know they love and support me."

"That's good. That's how family should be." Not that he had any experience, but he'd always imagined what it would be like, and what she'd said sounded exactly it.

When he took her fingers in his, she didn't pull away. The warmth flitted to his chest, filled his heart with possibilities. He didn't move, fearing he'd break the spell.

"It is how family should be," she agreed. "What about your parents? What kind of couple are they?"

For a moment, he considered deflecting her question, but he didn't want to do that to her, not when she was so honest and open with him. "I don't know," he told her. "I don't have any."

Emma kept her hand in his but leaned back to look at him straight on. "What do you mean?"

"Obviously, I know I have parents, or more accurately, I know there was a man and a woman who made me, but I never met them. Or if I did, I was too young to remember."

Her brow wrinkled in confusion and concern. "You're an orphan?"

"I was a foundling. Abandoned just after I turned one week old."

Her eyes widened. "Ryan, that is awful." She took both his hands in hers and gripped them tightly. "I'm so sorry."

Her reaction warmed his heart. "It's okay. I made peace with it a long time ago."

"No, of course it's not okay. Were you ever adopted? How did you grow up? Where?"

She turned his palm and laced her fingers with his. Was she even aware of what she was doing, how much that contact bolstered him, how much it healed the little cracks he'd been ignoring all his life?

"Tell me to stop if I'm being too nosy and insensitive." She hesitated. "If you don't want to talk about it, it's perfectly fine and I understand—"

He squeezed her hand. "You're not being too nosy and I don't mind talking about it." Not with her, he didn't.

She nodded, her expression encouraging, and he found he wanted to tell her everything.

"I grew up in foster care until I was sixteen and was never chosen for adoption. After a string of failed placements, I was sent to a group home as my last chance to shape up, and it changed my life. It was run by Hannah Sterling, but she went by Nana. That's what everybody called her. She gave me something I'd never had before—direction and encouragement to make my dreams into something worthwhile."

"Was that how you got started in your career?"

"It was a way to atone for my past mistakes. Nana repeated so many times that I could be whatever I wanted that I believed it. I got myself in physical shape and worked on my license from the Security Industry Administration, then applied to an organization that specializes in providing protection officers to high-profile principals."

"How did you end up with Royal Security?"

"For a chance at career advancement." He hesitated, then went on. "Not only for me, but to show those kids in situations like the one I had that it's possible to work for the future you want. But I couldn't have done it without Nana." He gazed at Emma. "I probably wouldn't be here right now if not for her."

"Did she adopt you?"

He shook his head. "No, I changed my name when I turned eighteen."

"So you never had a family?"

"Not officially, no."

She stared at him. "My goodness, the way you say that. Are you always so blasé when you tell your story?"

He swallowed. "You're the first one I've told it to, Emma." He drew a circle on the back of her hand with his thumb. "I've never shared so much with anyone else."

The weight of his declaration lay there between them, with Emma absorbing his words, or maybe trying to figure out what to say in return. He didn't know what to say, either, and let the silence stretch and turn to comfort, turn the connection into something tangible.

What magical powers did she have over him that he felt so comfortable with her and didn't mind being vulnerable?

"Thank you for telling me," she said at last. "Thank you for trusting me."

If only he could keep this feeling; if only he could keep her.

After a long minute between them, she asked, "How often do you see her?"

"Not often enough, and I'm due for a visit." When they returned, he'd find the time.

All too soon, the fire in the grate waned, reducing the room to near darkness.

Ryan edged away from Emma and stood to get the flashlight. He switched it on and handed it to her. "Why don't you go on ahead while I bank the coals?"

"What about you?"

"I'll use the oil lamp."

He took his time at the fireplace, making sure Emma had privacy to get ready for bed before he came upstairs.

While his past wasn't a secret, he'd never told anyone about it. It was part of his file at work, and Nana knew, of course, and so did a few of the kids who'd lived there around the same time, but no one else. It wasn't the kind of topic to bring up in professional relationships, the only kind he had. Without close friends and a family of his own, who else would he have talked with so candidly, shared so much of himself with?

But Emma had slipped into both roles effortlessly—a pretend wife who was more real than anyone else he'd had in his life in a long, long time. A close friend, his only family.

It felt right to share this part of himself with her, but in a way, it wasn't real. She was a Somerset princess, and he was her protection officer. When they returned to the palace, their lives would continue as before and nothing else. There was no future for them.

When he entered the attic bedroom, the flashlight sat upside down on the dresser and the beam pointed at the ceiling. Emma was already in bed. Had she fallen asleep yet?

Ryan damped the oil lamp and set it next to the flashlight, then turned off the flashlight as well. After his eyes adjusted to the darkness, he stepped gingerly on the creaky floorboards. At least the bed wouldn't be squeaking any more, not after the good tightening he'd given the springs earlier.

As he grabbed the pillow and quilt he'd used yesterday, Emma's voice cut the silence. "You're not sleeping on the floor tonight."

Not asleep, then.

She remained in the same position on her side, facing the dormer, and he couldn't see her expression.

"I'm fine," he said. "Don't worry about me."

"Maybe you're fine, but I'm not."

He stilled. What was he supposed to say to that? "Emma—"

"Please, Ryan," she whispered. "I can't let you sleep on the floor, and I can't be alone."

He wouldn't say no to her, not with that voice, not in that tone. Instead of lying on the floor, he took the pillow and stretched on top of the covers, keeping his distance from her.

Wordlessly, she turned around in bed and reached a hand out until she found his, then covered his fingers with her own. Not tightly like earlier, just a loose touch that said she was there.

She was there for him.

Chapter Seventeen

*E*mma glanced between Ryan and the ingredients gathered on the small table. "Are you sure you remember the recipe?"

"Trust me," he said with a confident grin. "This is the one recipe I know so well, I could make it in my sleep."

She read the recipe he'd written on a scrap of paper. "How are we going to make chocolate chip cookies without the chocolate chips and the vanilla extract?"

"They'll be chipless cookies." He picked up an old bottle. "Instead of vanilla, we'll use this beautifully aged brandy."

"If you're sure."

He pulled out a ceramic bowl from the cupboard. "Yes, I'm sure."

"Tell me what to do, then."

"Go ahead and measure the sugar while I cut the butter."

Emma followed his instructions one step at a time, and they worked together side by side. It was Friday after lunch, and it drizzled outside. Mary sat in the front room, knitting, and Tom dozed in the chair next to her.

Ryan had helped Emma with the dishes and had then offered to make cookies for after dinner. She liked this side of him, self-assured and happy to teach her, and she couldn't help but admire his willingness and positive attitude. The more time she spent with him, the more she enjoyed his company.

She'd wanted to take the little boy he'd been and scoop him up in a big, tight hug; she wanted to sit with the troublesome teenager and tell him he was important. Even after her parents had died, she'd never truly felt alone. She had a family, and she knew they loved her.

How could he have grown without people who loved him? How could he be the man he was today with that hole in his life? How had this man risen from a loveless childhood without deeper wounds to his soul? Whenever she thought about what he had told her the night before, she was in awe of everything he'd become.

Nana Sterling was her hero, and she wanted to hug the old lady too. Even without meeting her, Emma already knew she was a great woman.

Just as he'd told her, the cookies turned out delicious, despite the missing ingredients.

When she woke on Saturday morning, her mind turned to Ryan. She'd thought about his situation all day yesterday, through their chores at the cottage, playing with the dogs outside, baking cookies together in the small kitchen. Last night, as Emma had fallen asleep holding on to Ryan's hand again, the idea had burrowed in her mind. How many children were there in need of guidance and direction, like he'd been? In need of a safe place to stay, of a family to love them?

She'd been struggling for so long to find a way to make a difference, to champion a worthy cause, like Charlotte and Oliver did, and Alex, Stefan, and Henry. Aunt Nicolette had been nudging her, suggesting ideas, but none had felt right.

Until now.

Thoughts and ideas rushed through her, and she had to find a way to write them down.

Outside, the partly cloudy weather promised sunny skies for later. A good sign, but only for today. Once they returned to the palace, this magical time would end.

She found Mary in the kitchen.

"You're up early today," Mary said.

"I slept very well," Emma said. "The upstairs bed is growing on me." The company was as well. Too much so.

Hopefully he'd been more comfortable than on the floorboards their first night.

"I'm glad. I was worried you and Ryan wouldn't be comfortable. But you do know it's okay to sleep in on Saturday mornings, right?" She winked at Emma.

"Where are Tom and Ryan?"

"Ryan went out for his walk, and Tom is listening to the radio in the truck, even though I have one right here." She gestured at an old-fashioned radio sitting on a shelf, crooning from an oldies station.

Emma's eyes widened. "Wait. Is the power restored?"

"Yes, it is. Would you like to do a load of laundry?"

"I've never been happier for a chance to. Thank you, Mary."

While the laundry was washing, Emma helped Mary knead the dough for the daily bread, which would be ready by lunch. For breakfast, they had yesterday's leftover loaf. After, Mary went to collect the eggs from the chicken coop, and Emma watched from the outside.

"Do you want to give it a try?" Mary asked.

"Your chickens don't like me," Emma replied.

Mary laughed. "How do you know?"

"They're sending me death glares."

"You got to show them who's boss. That's all."

Emma shook her head. "I'd rather not deal with murderous chickens."

Later, when the bread was in the oven, Tom came in for breakfast, and Emma hung the wash on a line under the cover of the shed.

Ryan hadn't returned yet.

Emma stood at the small sink doing the breakfast dishes when she saw him emerging from the tree line. "Ryan's back," she said, her voice much too breathless.

Mary heard her nonetheless. "Go on, then. I can finish here." She smiled knowingly.

Emma wiped her hands on a dish towel and left through the back door, walking faster than she had to. The dogs had seen him, too, and came running to greet him, tails wagging as if they hadn't seen him just last night. That was how she felt. Exactly how she felt.

It had been too long.

When she came within the last few yards, she slowed. She slipped her hands in her pockets and smiled at Ryan, unsure how to greet him. "Good morning."

He gave the dogs one last pat and straightened to meet her eyes. "Good morning."

Before she lost her courage, Emma went on tiptoes and brushed a kiss on his cheek, so close to his mouth that she felt his smile at the corner.

"Mary's at the window," she offered as an explanation, certain he knew as well as she did it was only an excuse.

He nodded, still smiling. "She likes to look."

185

"Do you think they know about us?" she asked him.

"It's possible, but they haven't given any hints they do."

She and Ryan set out walking, side by side. Her hands remained in her pockets, the last thing she wanted. How easy it would be to reach for his hand.

"Any luck this morning?" she asked.

"I went in a different direction, but no cell signal. I don't know if it's because of the rain and floods or if it's normal for this area."

"The power came back," she told him.

"It won't do us any good without chargers and cords."

"Not for charging the phones, but I did a load of laundry in the wash, yours and mine."

"My jeans," he said longingly. "Thank you."

She chuckled. "You're welcome. I figured you've had enough of Tom's corduroy pants."

"It's better than going around in my underwear, and I'm glad he has something I can borrow, but I'm definitely ready to get my jeans back."

"Let's hope they dry quickly, then. Are you hungry? Would you like breakfast?"

"I had some coffee and toast before I left, thank you."

"Are you sure? I can make some eggs for you. It's going to be a while before lunch."

He cocked his head, his gaze intent on her, a half smile on his lips.

She frowned. "I thought you liked eggs."

"I do. Just about any kind."

"What's the hesitation, then?"

He watched her again. "You're not at all what I pegged you for when we met."

"Thank you. I guess?" Now she was curious. "Care to explain?"

"I mean it as a compliment. It's now Saturday, and we've been out here with the Baxters since Wednesday night with no power, no phone, and no luggage."

"And?"

He didn't reply right away. "And you haven't said anything."

"What should I have said?" But even as she asked, understanding dawned on her. "You thought I'd be complaining, didn't you? That's what you mean."

He glanced away for a second. "I admit I did. I had my doubts about you."

"You think I'm a spoiled princess," she said slowly. "Literally." Her shoulders dropped.

"It's not an excuse, but I didn't know you in the beginning. I don't think that of you now. I—"

"Hello, you Summers," Tom yelled from the kitchen door with a wave. "Come on over."

Emma waved back and raised her voice. "Coming, Tom."

187

"Emma—" Ryan started.

"Let's go see what Tom wants." She walked ahead, not waiting to see if he followed her.

Just a moment alone—the few yards it took to cross the remaining distance to the house—that was all she needed to process Ryan's words.

Did other people see her that way, as a woman who didn't appreciate what she had? Wasn't that what being spoiled meant?

Why did his good opinion of her matter so much? Or knowing with certainty that he thought the best of her?

She was only fooling herself. These feelings she'd been growing for him were obviously one sided. Being with her was his job, a duty, nothing more. Most likely, he was looking forward to returning to the palace and to their old routine, where everything would be normal again.

But Emma didn't want the old normal.

How crazy was that it she hadn't known he existed a month ago and now couldn't stop wishing they could stay at the Baxters' for another month, or even just one more week. These few days weren't enough. Not when she felt their inevitable end so sharply. Everything would be like it had been before too soon.

Emma brought a hand over her chest, willing her heart to calm down. Enough of these maudlin emotions that led nowhere.

She entered the kitchen with Ryan right behind her, and they found Tom waiting for them, Mary tending the stove.

"About time you get back," Tom said.

"Tom, let them have their time," Mary chided. "They're on their honeymoon."

If only.

Emma snuffed the thought. "Were the phone lines restored?"

"Not yet, but I heard on the radio the flood waters are receding in some places."

"That's good news," Ryan said. "Do you think we might have access to Blackwigg?"

"You won't know till you get there," Tom replied.

"Are you not coming?" Emma asked.

Tom waved a hand. "Nah, you two can handle it. You'll drive north for about ten or twelve miles until you see the river running parallel to the road. Slow down when you approach. The lower part of the road might still be underwater."

"If it is, don't try to cross," Mary said.

Tom nodded. "Aye. No crossing. Who knows what got dragged down there by the high waters. If it's good to cross, then Blackwigg is another three to four miles up the road. That's it."

"Whenever you're ready, I packed a light lunch for you." Mary nodded to a canvas bag sitting on the narrow counter. "Between here and Blackwigg there's a lookout that takes you to a view of the valley. It's worth the short detour and the drive there."

"A sightseeing detour?" Emma asked.

"Aren't you two still on your honeymoon?" Mary asked with a pointed look.

"Well, technically—" Ryan started.

"Technical or not, I don't see why you can't enjoy a little break and a picnic." Mary watched them both, but they didn't challenge her.

As awkward as it promised to be, how could they say no to that? Mary and Tom didn't know that she and Ryan had just had a disagreement. "Thank you, Mary," Emma replied.

"Here's the key." Tom handed it to Ryan. "I already filled the tank with the spare fuel I keep on hand for emergencies."

Emma chanced a look at Ryan and found the same bewilderment there.

"We'll get ready to go, then," Ryan said. "Thanks, Tom. Mary." He nodded at them.

Emma repeated the thanks, not knowing what else to say.

Ten minutes later, Emma walked to the truck at the end of the driveway where Ryan waited for her. She'd changed into her own clothes, washed and dried, and he wore his jeans and hoodie again. He held the passenger door for her, waited until she sat, went around and slipped in behind the wheel, then left.

She broke the silence first. "Did you get the impression they were trying to get rid of us?"

"You too?" He chuckled lightly. "They were so efficient about it."

"The keys, the full tank, the lunch."

"Right. All ready and waiting."

She glanced at him. "Maybe we've overstayed our welcome and they want their privacy back."

Ryan shook his head. "I don't think so. That's not the vibe I get from them."

"Something else, then."

"Yes, for sure, but I can't begin to think what."

"I can't either," Emma agreed.

Ryan drove confidently, and, despite their earlier tiff, sitting with him in the old truck felt familiar and comfortable, like something they did often. In Castlebridge, during her shopping outings, she sat in the back and he in the front, but side by side provided a kind of intimacy that brought a lightness to her heart.

After days of heavy rain and overcast skies, the sunny weather and wisps of white against the bright blue lent an air of hope, making it too easy to believe she was on vacation. But it wouldn't last much longer with the days getting shorter and shorter in their run toward fall. Just like their time here wouldn't last either.

How long would it take for the floods to recede, for things to go back to normal in this part of the country? How long for her life to return to the same routine she led at the palace?

More and more, she didn't want anything to be like before this trip. This was her new life. This simple living at the Baxters'—only her and Ryan—what more did she need, what else could she want? Not much.

If it weren't for her family, and the worry they must be feeling for not knowing where she was, Emma wouldn't mind staying. For a little while longer, at least.

They easily found the turn off, just as the Baxters had told them. The worn road serpentined through the trees, gradually climbing, until it ended in a clearance with a rocky outcropping and a view without obstructions.

Ryan parked the truck and they exited.

A sea of foliage rolled out in front of them, from green to gold to orange, undulating and alive, as far as they could see. The river wasn't visible from here, and Blackwigg was probably hiding under the tree canopy to the west.

"Mary was right," Emma said. "It's a beautiful view."

"Worth the detour," Ryan agreed.

She found a fallen log and sat down.

When he joined her, he brought the canvas bag with the lunch Mary had packed them, with an assortment of cold meats, cheese, bread, and boiled eggs, with apple cider in a bottle.

"It almost seems crazy, don't you think?" Emma asked.

"What?"

She nodded toward the view before them. "It's so quiet and peaceful. Easy to forget there are floods out there, loss of power and communication. People displaced, or even worse."

"Do you feel unsafe?"

"Not all." She paused for a moment before continuing. "We have delicious food and an amazing view, and it's enough. I could stay here and be happy. It's a selfish thought, I know," she added.

"It would be easy to be happy here."

They ate in companionable silence until most of the food was gone, and Emma tried to bottle the moments of enjoyment, the view and the weather, and especially the man sitting next to her.

When they were done, Ryan stood and held out his hand. "We should get going, before it gets too dark."

She hesitated for a moment but then took his hand and let him help her up from the log, unable to resist enjoying the feel of his hand in hers as long as she could. They cleaned after themselves, returned to the truck, and set out to the main road.

Ryan glanced twice at her. "I'm sorry for what I said this morning when you came out to meet me."

"I'm sorry I overreacted. There's nothing to apologize for, Ryan. You didn't say anything to offend me."

"Maybe so, but my words hurt you, and that wasn't my intention."

"They didn't hurt as much as they made me think. Have you ever had a moment of self-realization about something that never occurred to you before?"

He kept his eyes ahead and frowned lightly. "Yeah, I have."

"What you said really made me think," she admitted. "I'm not independent, and I can't go anywhere alone because my uncle is the king of Durham. Whether I like it or not, I'm a public figure, and people will think what they want of me. I know that. I've always known that, but I truly don't remember considering I might be viewed as a brat."

"I really didn't—" His eyes widened. "Oh boy."

Emma turned to look out the windshield. A herd of cows filled the road ahead, packed tightly from side to side. Not just any cows, but brown ones with woolly hair, some with curved horns and some without. Nothing but cows in the middle of the road.

"How are we going to pass by them?" she asked.

Chapter Eighteen

*R*yan cursed under his breath. He put the truck in reverse to get some distance between them and the herd, then slipped the gear into park and got out.

"Stay inside," he told Emma.

He'd been talking to her and got distracted, didn't anticipate what came after the curve in the road until he was nearly upon it. About fifty cows, maybe more, stood in the middle of the road, lowing. Where had they come from? He couldn't see anyone tending to them.

The passengerside door opened and closed, and Emma came to join him at the front of the truck.

He touched the spot between his eyes. "Do you always do the opposite of what you're asked to do?"

She frowned at him. "It's a herd of cows. How dangerous can they be?" After a moment of watching the animals, she asked, "What are they waiting for?"

"For a way to get to higher ground. They're trapped."

The road took a dip after the curve and, as the Baxters had said, the west side ran parallel to the river and was still underwater.

"There must be pasture fields to the east, through this line of trees." He gestured to the side. "The cows must have come through there, or from down the road, and stopped when they found the water."

"Will they be able to pass?" Emma asked.

"I don't think so, but I really don't know anything about cows."

"I hope they'll be okay."

"I'm sure they will. Someone will notice them missing and come looking for them." He turned back to the truck. "Let's go, Emma. We can't continue on to Blackwigg. Even if the cows weren't here, the road is still flooded."

Unless the phone line was restored in the next few hours, they'd be spending another night at the Baxters', and most likely another day as well.

What was the protocol for a missing princess? Was there an official search by the Royal Security guard, or were they keeping her disappearance under wraps? Without any clues left behind as a lead, Royal Security had no way of knowing where he and Emma had gone on Wednesday morning, and he didn't know if the car tracker could provide any information. It would be near impossible to set up search parameters that could result in any kind of rescue. What about the consequences for him? Would he be fired for not letting anyone know where he and Emma had gone?

Ryan came around to the passengerside door and held it open for Emma. As she made her way across the field, an enormous black dog charged from the underbrush and zeroed in on her, barking menacingly. She screamed and ran back the way she'd come. She jumped, grasping on to a low branch of the nearest tree on the bank, then scrambled up faster than he would have believed. Emma settled on a branch well out of reach of the dog, even as the animal tried to jump up at her.

"Hang on," Ryan yelled. He looked around and found a large stick, intent on scaring the beast away.

But between the dog and him, the commotion proved too much for the herd—the cows took off, stampeding haphazardly down the road, in the opposite direction of the flooded area. Ryan hunkered down on the other side of the truck as everything around him shook.

As the last cow passed him by, he sprinted toward the tree. The dog was gone, probably spooked by the herd, and Emma hung on to the trunk, eyes scrunched closed. It shouldn't have surprised him that she knew how to climb trees. Every time he believed he was beginning to understand her, she went and did something unexpected.

"Emma," he called up to her. "It's safe to come down now."

He took a step back and assessed the situation, not liking what he saw. The tree wasn't a large, sturdy one, and it stood too close to the riverbank, partly leaning over the raging waters.

Her voice came a moment later. "Is the dog gone?"

"The dog is gone and the cows are gone. It's just you and me. Let's get you down, please."

"I can't move. I'm afraid I'll fall in the river if the branch breaks."

Given the position of the tree, and how full the river was, the possibility of that happening was a real one, so real it frightened him.

"I know it's scary, Emma, but you have to trust me," he said in a firm, gentle tone. "I'm going to guide you down. Just listen to my voice."

Little by little, Emma followed his directions until she reached a lower branch. Ryan watched from below, his heart in his throat every time she moved, every time the tree made a cricking sound. Never had he felt this powerless, so helpless and unable to do more for her.

"Good job, Emma. You're doing great," he encouraged. "Now you're going to sit sideways on that branch, facing me."

"I don't know if I can do this," came her tense reply, barely audible.

"Yes, you can," he pled. "I'm right here, and I won't leave you. Just listen to my voice. Can you hear me and do that?"

"Yes."

The longer she spent on the tree, the harder it would be to get her down. With her mental state getting more precarious, the daylight waning and the temperature dropping, the chances of something going terribly wrong were climbing by the minute.

"Emma, listen to me. Put your right hand out on the tree trunk for support." Slowly, she did. "Now lower yourself down. You can do it—I know you can."

Out of the corner of his eye, he watched a threat approaching, a massive tree trunk floating rapidly on the river, scraping along the bank toward the tree where Emma still sat, paralyzed with fear.

"Jump, Emma," Ryan yelled. "Jump now."

She let go with a scream. He grabbed her in a tackle by her midsection, dropped on the ground, and rolled her on top of him, his hold on her tight as she cried on his chest.

"I've got you," he whispered in her ear. "I've got you."

With a deafening sound, the floating trunk hit the branches where Emma had been just a moment before, taking part of the live tree with it, part of the bank crumbling away.

He closed his eyes and hugged her closer.

The thought chilled him, how close he'd come to losing her. He couldn't—not physically, and not for the sake of his own heart.

Chapter Nineteen

$\mathcal{E}$mma woke with the sound of the door squeaking open, and she turned to look.

Ryan poked his head in. "I'm sorry. I didn't mean to wake you. I forgot to oil these hinges."

"It's okay. You can come in. What time is it?"

"Just after eight." He sat at the foot of the bed.

"In the morning?" She dragged herself into a sitting position and rubbed her eyes.

"No, in the evening. You slept for a couple hours."

"Feels like I've been sleeping for days." Napping in the afternoon sometimes gave her a sense of disorientation upon waking up.

"You needed the rest," Ryan said, softly. "How are you feeling?"

The memories of what had happened earlier rushed to her. "Thanks to you, I'm fine."

If Ryan hadn't caught her, she would have fallen into the choppy waters. Seeing part of the riverbank crumble after the log came barreling down, taking most of the tree she'd climbed on with it, had been too much to process, what with the dog's near attack and the cows trampling the road—too many things happening, too many emotions all at once. She'd been unable to stop the tears, the shock causing a heightened reaction.

Ryan had driven them back to the Baxters', where Mary had put her to bed with a cup of tea to calm her nerves and help the trembling stop. Fortunately, she'd fallen asleep.

Emma closed her eyes for a moment. "I'm so sorry, Ryan. I never meant to put us in danger."

"I know you didn't."

"That dog came out of nowhere, and he was aimed right at me," she recounted. "I barely had time to react. I don't know what made me go up that tree." It had all happened so fast.

Ryan shifted and sat closer. "You don't have to think about it. It's over."

Tears of frustration flooded her eyes and she wiped at them angrily. "And now I'm crying like a brat."

Ryan reached for her hand. "That's not what I see. You're not a brat. I've been accompanying you and watching what you do, and you're a kind person, Emma."

Emma turned fully to him. Did he really see her as more than the princess under his protection? The heat of his fingers on hers sent a current up her arm, and her heart tripped.

"When you went shopping, you were kind to all the employees and even to those girls who tried to get a selfie with you."

"They were American and didn't know about the protocol in Durham. I couldn't be mean to them for something they didn't understand."

"On the tour, you always smiled and thanked all the teachers and nurses and personnel, and you always gave individual attention to the children, making them feel important. Even if it was just a smile and a word of encouragement, a small touch."

"Children *are* important," she insisted. "Everything you're saying is a part of my duties in public. It doesn't make me special."

"It's much more than that. You always go above and beyond your duty. Your kindness is personal, not fake. You do the same with the Baxters. You help around the house and the yard, you listen to them, you thank them."

"They've been the most gracious hosts. They deserve all the thanks. Besides, I couldn't very well expect them to wait on me. I'm incognito, remember?"

Ryan sighed. "Incognito or not, your attitude is the same. You're kind, you respect people, and you are special." After a small pause, he continued, his voice lower, more intimate. "I was so worried about you today. If anything had happened . . ."

The implication hung between them.

Emma patted the quilt with her free hand and picked up a non-existent piece of lint. She couldn't look at Ryan. Had he really been watching her so closely all this time, noticing who she really was?

"You're my protection officer. Of course you're going to worry about me and say nice things about me." She let her hair tumble, a curtain between them, hopefully hiding her red cheeks. "It's your job to do both."

Her heart raced, and her palms were too warm and perspired. She kept her eyes from him. He'd see it there—he'd see this attraction she'd been growing for him. If he looked at her, she wouldn't be able to hide anything from him.

When he didn't reply, she dared a peek. "Ryan?"

He caught her gaze. One of his hands brushed away the hair from her face. "You're not a spoiled princess, Emma Somerset. And I wasn't worried about you because I'm your protection officer."

"But you are," she protested weakly.

The corner of his mouth went up a little at her persistence. "I was worried because I care about you. You, Emma. Not you, the princess I was hired to protect, but you, the woman I admire."

He cared about her? Admired her?

At her hesitation and doubt, he tipped his head and leaned closer. "What must I do for you to believe me?"

As she struggled to find the words to reply, to voice the questions and reservations she still had, Ryan didn't wait.

Gently, he brought his hands to frame her face, and his deep brown eyes searched hers for a brief moment. When he found the answer he needed, he touched his mouth to hers. Not a brief quasi kiss like before; not on the corner of her lips, but exactly on her mouth in a perfect match.

Wanting him closer, her arms came around his neck, and she slipped onto the mattress. Ryan brought an arm around her shoulders, palmed the side of her face, and when she parted her lips for a better fit, he deepened the kiss in a decadent rush. His body fell on the bed next to hers, their shoulders and chests, their hips and legs aligned. Heat rippled through her in a wave of goose bumps, and any shred of rational thought vanished immediately.

Nothing else mattered.

He tasted of cinnamon and sugar, the cookies Mary had made for tea, and smelled of lemon soap, the kind the Baxters kept in their shower. His hair was soft and still damp, and Emma ran her fingers through it, then touched the skin at the back of his neck in lazy circles.

With the other hand, she touched his chin, ran her palm along his jawline and the beard he hadn't shaved since Wednesday, so different from his clean-faced look at the palace.

The kiss turned into a series of long kisses. Give, take, breathe.

Give, take, breathe.

On and on and on.

How long had she been yearning for this kiss? She hadn't admitted it before, not for the blink of a moment, and not even to herself, but she'd wanted to touch him and kiss him for some time, for what felt like forever. A deep longing that burned even brighter now made her want him even more after having a taste of him.

She brought her hand to his side, under his T-shirt, and touched his skin, ran her fingers through the taut muscles there.

Ryan sucked in a breath. Immediately, he let go of her, and sat up on the edge of the mattress. "I'm sorry, Emma." Another ragged breath. "That was inappropriate."

Inappropriate?

Emma sat up in bed as well, dazed, confused, keenly missing his lips on her mouth, his body next to hers, his hands touching her. How could he be sorry? Did he regret kissing her?

She reached out her hand. "Ryan, please—"

"Dinner will be ready in ten minutes," Mary hollered from the bottom of the stairs.

Ryan sprang from the side of the bed as if they'd been caught in a compromising position. Weren't they posing as a married couple? It wouldn't be compromising. He rubbed his neck and exhaled deeply, then looked over his shoulder at her. "I'm going down to help. Take as much time as you need."

Emma let her hair fall in front of her eyes again. "I'll be right there."

After he left, she scrubbed her face with her hands. Just her luck; Mary had the worst timing ever.

Emma had been about to tell Ryan he didn't have to apologize. Of course he didn't. How was she going to let him understand this week had been the best time of her life? No royal duties, no social pressures, no public eye judging her every move—nothing was better than their stay with the Baxters these past few days. Nothing could even compare. Almost like a normal life. Even the lack of electricity and phone had helped the atmosphere in the house and between them, bringing them closer.

After dinner, she would talk to him.

She had to. Their return to the palace couldn't be the end of things between them; it had to be the beginning somehow.

Chapter Twenty

*R*yan woke with a start, a crick on the stairs cutting the silence.

He moved Emma's hand from his arm and quietly got up, opening the door only as wide as he dared. A few steps below stood Tom, still dressed in pajama bottoms and a tank top, the light from the hallway below casting a long shadow. Ryan followed him down the stairs, and they stopped at the bottom landing.

"I thought you'd like to know," Tom said. "The phone lines have been restored."

"Just now?" Ryan asked.

Tom nodded. "The council in Blackwigg is calling all the folks in the area to check on them. Access roads are still flooded."

Ryan scrubbed his face. "What time is it?"

"Just after six in the morning." Tom gestured to the wall behind them. "The phone is over there, in the alcove."

"Thanks, Tom."

Tom returned to his bedroom, and Ryan walked to the kitchen for a glass of water.

It was early enough that the sun hadn't yet peeked, but it wouldn't be much longer. He stood at the window over the sink, formulating a plan—call the palace, wait for instructions, wake up Emma and tell her.

A twinge of regret pricked his conscience.

He and Emma hadn't had the chance to talk last night after he kissed her. Instead, the Baxters had called them for dinner, and during the meal, she'd looked at him with a question in her gaze, one that beckoned for conversation. After their usual post meal time in front of the fireplace with Tom and Mary, Emma had helped clean up, and he'd gone to the garage to fix the broken side-view mirror, a casualty of the stampede and more of an excuse to avoid time alone with her than a pressing matter. By the time he'd returned inside, she'd already fallen asleep.

How would he find the time to talk to her today? How would he apologize for kissing her or explain why he'd done it? If she even wanted to listen to him.

He filled the kettle and put it on, then lit the gas burner. The Baxters didn't have a coffee machine, and the boiled water would work for both tea and coffee. This morning, he needed a cup of strong brew to face the day.

The phone was an old rotary one, almost an antique, from times when life had been much simpler. Only a few days ago, Ryan had carried his own cell phone with him at all times and had constantly checked it for messages. Now he didn't care if he ever saw it again, didn't even want to use it. But it was time to return to his regular life, to his old normal.

He called the number he'd memorized in his first week at the palace.

"Security central," came the voice on the other side.

"This is Protection Officer Ryan Sterling." He rattled off his credential numbers for verification.

"Stand by."

Ryan waited, the minutes ticking.

"Sterling, is that really you?" It was Chief Officer Peters, the head of security.

"Yes, sir, it's me." Ryan repeated his credential numbers.

"Yes, yes," CO Peters said impatiently. "Your identity was verified. Where have you been? And more importantly, where is Her Highness, and how is she faring?"

"Her Highness is here with me, and she's doing well. We got stranded on Wednesday and haven't had access to a phone until this morning."

"Let me pull up the satellite map, and you're going to tell me your exact location."

Ryan did as asked, explaining the drive to Hillside Meadows, the flooding river, the bridge collapse, how Tom Baxter had picked them up. He kept it succinct for now; he'd save the details for his written report.

"What about this little village, Blackwigg?" CO Peters asked.

"The road is flooded, sir. We couldn't get through, still can't."

After a pause, CO Peters said, "Can I call you back at this number?"

"Yes, sir." Ryan replied. "I'll be here."

The logistics would take time. He'd never been in a situation like this, but many similar ones, where extracting a principal from somewhere risky had been imperative. After the past few days away from civilization, with only Emma and the Baxters for company, he'd easily fallen in a new routine, almost believing their cover.

All of this ended today. No more sharing a room, a bed, a life as Emily Summers's husband. He and Emma were going back to their roles of protection officer and principal.

Only his principal was Her Royal Highness Princess Emma Somerset.

And he was well on his way to falling in love with her, if not there already.

Ryan let out a long breath.

What had he done with that kiss?

Impatience flared as he waited for the return call, which was taking too long.

Ryan couldn't leave the phone until the call came, a small inconvenience nobody was used to anymore. He'd wake up Emma once he knew what the plans were; he'd let her sleep until then.

When the phone rang, Ryan grabbed the receiver with the first ring. "Sterling here," he said.

"Peters here. After studying the conditions in the area, and with the goal of bringing Her Royal Highness home as soon as possible, we decided the best course of action is to send the helicopter for her." Peters explained the rendezvous point. "You'll need to bring Princess Emma to this location."

"Yes, sir," Ryan replied.

"This helicopter is being deployed for His Royal Highness Prince Alexander's use and can only accommodate four at a time. If his schedule permits, it'll go back for you later in the day. If not, we'll send a car."

"Very well, sir." With the pilot, Prince Alexander, and his protection officer, there would only be room for Emma.

"Sterling, they're already en route. Forty-five minutes, an hour at the most. Don't make them wait."

"Yes, sir."

CO Peters hung up, and Ryan put down the receiver.

"Did I hear the phone ringing?"

Emma stood at the bottom of the stairs, still wearing the borrowed nightgown, no socks, her braid loose over her shoulder. His eyes focused on her bare feet, and his heart stumbled. Of all the things to rob his attention, the sight of her naked toes on the old floor planks shouldn't be it. There was so much more. This life they'd lived the past few days, this alternate reality that felt nothing but authentic—this was the end. No more.

"Ryan?" Emma asked.

He shook himself mentally, brought his eyes up to hers. "Yes, the phone line was restored a little while ago."

"Who was that on the phone?"

"Chief Officer Peters." Ryan suppressed a long exhale. "You're going home."

Chapter Twenty-One

"What do you mean, I'm going home?"

Emma took a step closer to Ryan but paused when he crossed his arms over his chest. His demeanor had changed. Although his voice wasn't harsh, there was a lack of warmth in his body language, in his eyes. Something was wrong. Was this about the kiss yesterday?

"I called the palace security after Tom told me the phone was working." His eyes kept wandering, as if he couldn't face her. "CO Peters called me back with the plan to get you home today."

"Today? How soon?"

"In about forty-five minutes." He moved past her into the kitchen, avoiding coming too close. "Let me get dressed first, then you can take your turn. We need to leave soon. I made a fresh pot of coffee." He gestured at the old-fashioned coffeepot.

"Sure. Thank you."

He returned in less than five minutes. Barely enough time to pour the coffee in a mug. She retreated to the attic bedroom, closed the door behind her, and leaned against the old wood.

Something was wrong, but it was her fault to expect so much after one kiss. A series of kisses, really. Why had she expected his heart only because she'd given him hers? She'd assumed so much about this morning, had dreamed about it all night—whispered confessions, moments alone, all the kisses.

Instead of dreaming of her like she had of him, Ryan had changed his mind. It was the only explanation for his cold behavior. And who was she to fault him?

She quickly dressed, stripped the bed and gathered all the laundry in a bundle, and then went looking for the Baxters. She owed them an apology and an explanation.

When Emma arrived back in the kitchen, Ryan was gone, but Mary was there. She pushed the cup of coffee toward Emma, with a thick slice of rustic bread slathered in homemade butter.

"Good morning, dear," Mary said. "I'd have made you something more substantial but Ryan said you're leaving soon. Hope this is enough."

The lady's eyes said everything—in such a small house, she and Tom had no doubt heard Ryan on the phone.

Emma dropped the bundle on the floor and hugged her new friend. "Oh, Mary. I'm sorry for all the lies. You and Tom have been the most gracious hosts, and I didn't even tell you my real name."

"Don't fret, dear. We know you didn't do it out of malice." Mary patted Emma's back and pulled away. "Your safety is important. Sit down and eat while you have time."

Emma picked up the laundry. "Let me run this to the washer. I'd planned to clean the bedroom and put the laundry away, but I won't have the time." She winced. "I'm sorry, Mary. I didn't mean to leave all this work for you."

"Pishposh," Mary said with a wave of her hand. "You're the princess, dear. I shouldn't have let you help in the first place, but it wasn't my place to say anything."

Emma took a bite of her toast. She didn't want to argue with Mary and tell her that being the princess shouldn't excuse her from helping. Other people would accuse her of taking advantage of her privilege for much less.

"Have you seen Ryan?" Emma asked.

"He said he was going to check the truck."

He must be waiting for her. Emma quickly finished her coffee and toast and thanked Mary for the breakfast. They walked through the house and found Ryan and Tom in the drive, the dogs beside them, all of them by the truck.

"Tom, how can I ever thank you for picking us up on the side of the road last Wednesday? You saved us."

"No thanks necessary," Tom said in his usual way. "It was my pleasure, Your Highness."

"Please, none of that. It's Emma to you and Mary." She gave him a quick hug. "You're my good friends. No titles necessary."

"Brutus and Nero," Emma said to the dogs. At hearing their names, they approached her, tails wagging and tongues lolling. "Goodbye, you silly dogs." She laughed at their antics.

With each word, each hug and goodbye, her composure slipped, tears already threatening. Four days had passed too quickly but, in a way, had felt like a lifetime, a parallel life of which she wanted more. So much more.

Ryan opened the passenger door for her. After one last look at the hill, the cottage, and the Baxters, Emma waved goodbye and got in.

"Wait. Isn't Tom coming?" she asked Ryan after he started the truck.

"No, I'm driving you."

"But how are the Baxters getting the truck back?"

"I'll drive it back," Ryan said.

Her chest tightened. "You're not coming back to the palace?"

"Not right now. There's no room."

She frowned. "I don't understand."

"I'm driving you to meet the helicopter that Prince Alexander is already using for official business in the area. It's a four seater."

She counted. "The pilot, Alex, and his protection officer."

"Yes," Ryan confirmed.

"How are you coming back, then?"

"They'll return for me."

Did she imagine the tension behind his words despite his casual tone? "Will I see you tonight?"

He glanced at her with a small smile. "I'm sure you will."

Somehow, it didn't reassure her.

Ten minutes later, Ryan parked on the side of the road. A clearing in the trees opened to the east and would afford the space the helicopter needed to land.

"They should be here soon," Ryan said, after a few moments.

It was his calm, professional tone, the one he'd used with her when they'd first met in Aunt Nicolette's office and during that whole first week of shopping trips to the city. Was that only two weeks ago?

Time was a peculiar element, playing tricks on her mind, on her perception of others and of herself. The weeks and days were there, marked on the calendar, on the passing of each day, but the hours and minutes were in her heart, augmenting and shrinking in non linear time. It hadn't been too long since she'd met him, but she couldn't imagine a life without him.

Emma opened the door and got out of the truck.

Ryan immediately followed her. "Emma. Please."

She walked away. "I need some air," she said over her shoulder. She wouldn't go too far, of course. Just some distance to think, to clear her mind and get used to the idea of returning to the palace.

"Let's wait in the car. It's safer when the helicopter comes. Emma," he called again.

At least he still used her first name. That wouldn't continue once they returned.

She turned around and faced Ryan, her hands in her pockets. He paused and didn't come any farther, the hesitation clear.

Maybe she'd confront him, ask him why he was treating her so reservedly. Was it because they were going back, or was there something more? What about that kiss they'd shared?

The whirring of helicopter blades approached, first faintly, until it filled the space above them, wind displacing everything around, hastening the drop of so many leaves that still clung to their branches.

As she stood watching it land, her hands taming her hair in vain, Ryan grabbed her elbow and leaned closer.

Was he going to kiss her? Her heart tumbled in anticipation.

"Bend," he said in her ear, already propelling her to the helicopter.

Alex's protection officer jumped out, ducking his head and holding the door open for them. Before she had time to think it through, Ryan handed her in, and Alex pulled her inside on the seat next to him.

"It's so good to see you, Emma." Alex hugged her, then placed a headset on her.

"Great to see you too, Alex." Emma looked outside to say goodbye to Ryan, but he was already walking away toward Tom's truck.

Alex's protection officer jumped back in, and the helicopter left.

"We've all been worried about you, especially Mother," Alex went on.

She glanced out again. Ryan stood by the truck looking up, already too far away to see his expression.

It felt wrong to leave him behind.

Alex kept talking, and she tried to focus on him, holding her hands in her lap to stop from fidgeting. She blinked hard to fight the tears forming against her will. How ridiculous to miss Ryan so much already, to be this sad their time together was over.

Once back at the palace, Uncle Geoffrey and Aunt Nicolette walked toward Emma as soon as she landed and embraced her as she entered the courtyard.

"You're home at last," Aunt Nicolette said. "We've been worried about you," she echoed Alex's words of earlier.

"We're so glad you're safely home," Uncle Geoffrey added.

"I am too." Not a complete lie. There were many good things about being home. And one spectacularly hard thing about being back too.

Ryan.

Or Mr. Sterling, as he would likely prefer to be called upon his return.

She had much to think about, much to ponder of what had happened over the last few days. Already, she missed having Ryan at her side. When would she see him next?

Aunt Nicolette continued talking as they made their way to Emma's apartment.

"Dear," Uncle Geoffrey interrupted. "Why don't we leave her to take a shower and get a good breakfast, and come back later?"

He kissed Emma's brow and took Aunt Nicolette's hand in his.

Emma thanked him, then kissed them both and assured Aunt she would meet them for lunch.

Once inside, she locked the door and sighed. Good Uncle Geoffrey always knowing the best way to defuse her Aunt's over-zealousness. She meant well, Emma knew that, but she could be too forceful in her attentions.

Emma plugged her battery-dead phone into the charger and then took a slow shower, grateful for the water pressure and all the comforts she'd always taken for granted. She'd appreciated the Baxters' hospitality, but it wasn't the same as being home. The thought made her feel ungrateful, spoiled. There was that word again.

There must be something she could do to show her gratitude to Tom and Mary. Something appropriate and needed for the home, along with a heartfelt, personal thank-you note. Maybe a generator and fuel, so they wouldn't be without power next time there was an emergency.

And what would she do for Ryan? Yes, it was his job to protect her, but he'd done more than that. He'd been her friend, and friendship didn't have a price. She'd have to come up with the perfect way to thank him. Something meaningful, if she could ever find it.

But before that, she had to talk to him—they couldn't continue with their lives as before the trip. She didn't want that and hoped he didn't either. And that kiss. Had it even meant anything to him as it had to her?

Her luggage from the trip had been returned, and she unpacked and put it away while taking a light meal Aunt Nicolette had arranged.

Once her phone had enough battery charge, she dialed Charlotte's number for a video call.

"Emma," her cousin said, waving enthusiastically. "You're back."

"I am back." Emma waved.

"Mother texted me this morning when they got word. We've been worried."

"I've heard, but I'm okay. Nothing happened," Emma assured Charlotte.

"Nothing happened? You disappeared without a trace."

"When you put it that way, I guess we did. We never meant to," she added.

"Tell me," Charlotte asked.

"We went sightseeing, and the location was more remote than we realized," Emma started. She told Charlotte about the flooding river, the bridge collapse, the back tires popping. "We couldn't call for help without cell coverage, and we didn't know it was because of the floods or the area not having coverage. Luckily, a truck stopped for us on this country road. I used a made-up name, and then Ryan came up beside me and introduced himself as my husband."

Charlotte's eyes widened, and her voice went up. "Your what?"

Emma lowered her voice. "Don't tell your parents, please. I *don't* want to get Ryan in trouble. He told Tom Baxter we were newlyweds."

"So he could be with you all the time," Charlotte added.

Emma nodded. "Yes, that was his idea. We wanted to go to the village, but the access road was flooded, so the Baxters invited us to stay with them."

"Is that where you were this whole time?"

"Yes, in Tom and Mary Baxter's home. The electricity and phone lines were down, and we still couldn't call anyone, but at least we had a place to sleep and food to eat."

"My goodness," Charlotte said, "what a rustic adventure. Was it very bad?"

Emma paused, watching her cousin on the small screen. "It was wonderful, Char. If it weren't for the flood, and knowing the family was concerned for me, it would have been perfect." She told Charlotte about the nights in front of the fire, the long talks, cooking and cleaning together, learning to slow down and enjoy the small things. The lack of pressure, no public eye judging every little thing she did.

Charlotte smiled. "I think it was Ryan's company. Your fake husband." She did air quotes with her fingers.

"I—"

"Don't deny it, Emma Somerset." Charlotte wagged her finger. "I can see the stars in your eyes and the blush in your cheeks."

Emma let out a deep sigh. "No, I won't deny it. Ryan is wonderful." He made everything better.

"And you're in love with him."

Was she? "I've known him for a little over two weeks, Char," she argued. "How is that possible?"

"Oh, it's possible all right. Does he return your feelings?"

"It sounds pathetic, but I don't know."

Charlotte frowned. "Did you kiss? Did you talk?"

"We talked, we kissed and then we didn't have a chance to talk again," Emma admitted. "It's complicated."

"Why? Because he's your PPO?"

"There must be a rule about it somewhere, don't you think?" Emma asked.

"If there's one, I'll find out."

"Be careful what you say and who you ask," Emma rushed to add. "I don't want any problems for Ryan or his career. I mean it."

"I'll be discreet, Em, you can trust me. In the meantime, you two should talk. Clear the air between you."

Emma nodded, then veered the conversation away from Ryan and asked Charlotte about the baby, all the while still thinking about him. After hanging up, Emma pulled out her laptop and turned it on. She didn't keep social media apps on her phone and didn't like checking the news either. But curiosity got the better of her—what had the media published about her last week? She and Ryan had already been one of the hot topics after that photo had been published, the one that had caught them staring at each other outside the hospital in Meeds.

She searched for the main news outlets only; the gossip rags weren't worth the trouble and time. As she'd expected, most of the articles had been published on Thursday, when her entourage didn't arrive in Inverly, the last destination in her trip.

Headlines abounded about the missing princess, some insinuating she and Ryan were spending time together, others bluntly suggesting they had eloped. She skipped the comments; those would be even worse.

Maggie Stanton, the senior press secretary for the palace, had issued a public statement an hour after Emma's return, saying the princess was back with her family, and thanking her protection officer for keeping her safe. The statement didn't mention Ryan by his name, and it didn't have any details of where they'd been, notwithstanding the questions in the comments. Why were people on social media so nosy and demanding?

Maybe it was best to lie low, away from public scrutiny, until something more bombastic came along to take center stage. She wasn't worried for herself, but what about Ryan? How did he feel about all this? Had he made it back yet? Would she have the courage to talk to him?

How was she going to face him and go on as before, without reaching for his hand?

Chapter Twenty-Two

$\mathcal{R}$yan held his hand in a fist, then caught himself and relaxed his fingers. It wouldn't do if anyone saw him and thought he had an anger management problem. He had to keep calm, maintain his neutral behavior and appearance, especially when he met with the queen.

He'd arrived back at the palace yesterday in the late afternoon after catching a ride in Prince Alexander's helicopter. Following a short meeting with Chief Officer Peters and his team supervisor, Ryan had collected his luggage from the trip and had returned to his apartment. He'd looked around the small space and had been immediately hit with a sense of incompletion, an ache in his chest for Emma.

He missed her so much it sent him reeling.

He missed sitting across the table from her at meals, missed their times on the sofa in front of the fireplace, especially missed sharing that small bed with her in the loft.

As comfortable as his bed was here, he didn't sleep well, not without Emma breathing deeply and sleeping inches away from him as she had at the Baxters' cottage, her hand resting on his arm.

And that kiss. He couldn't put it out of his mind. She'd felt so right in his arms, even as he knew he shouldn't feel that way.

This morning, he'd made the mistake of looking at the news. The media had been relentless about Emma's disappearance. So many insinuations about her and him. It enraged him.

Now, on his way to Queen Nicolette's office, Ryan had let his resentment and antagonism for the press get the best of him for a moment. He couldn't let his feelings get to him like that.

He stopped in front of the door, then took a deep breath, squared his shoulders, and knocked.

Mr. Poe, the queen's secretary, opened the door and announced him.

"Come in, Mr. Sterling," Queen Nicolette said. "Thank you for coming."

Ryan bowed from the neck. "Your Majesty."

She stood from her desk and came around to meet him. "I'd like to personally offer my thanks to you for looking after Emma and keeping her safe. His Majesty as well."

"Thank you, ma'am." Ryan inclined his head.

"Regardless of responsibility and duty, Mr. Sterling, your dedication and commitment didn't go unnoticed and are deeply appreciated."

He repeated his thanks and bowed to Her Majesty.

Once back in the hallway, Ryan's shoulders dropped with guilt. He'd taken care of Emma much too well. What would Queen Nicolette say if she knew he'd kissed her niece? For sure, she wouldn't thank him.

As he turned the corner, he found Emma approaching from the access to the family wing. She stopped at the sight of him, watching him, holding her hands clasped in the front, as if deciding what to do. For a moment, he thought she'd turn around and leave. When she stayed in the same spot—was she waiting for him?—he shortened the distance between them until he stood in front of her, keeping the protocol distance. This area wasn't private, what with the security cameras, and they could be interrupted at any time by employees.

"Good morning, Princess Emma," he greeted.

"Good morning, Mr. Sterling," she replied.

She wore a pair of tapered pants and a blouse, an outfit that wasn't formal enough for official business but was miles away from the casual clothes she'd worn at the Baxters'. It was the other side of her, the one before and during the trip. While at their stay with Tom and Mary, she'd been different, casual, free. She'd been Emma, not the princess.

His fingers itched to touch her, to feel her skin on his, to put his arm around her waist and draw her closer for a slow kiss.

He clasped his hands behind his back.

"How have you been, ma'am?" he asked.

"I'm well, thank you. Did you get back without incident?"

"Yes, ma'am, everything went well."

The current awkwardness between them made the loss of what they'd had before sharper, but he couldn't risk more at the palace, not when his career and Emma's reputation could be made to suffer. Would it always be like this, stilted exchanges and downcast eyes, ignoring that they'd ever had a measure of intimacy that came easy and natural?

A pause ensued, the unease floating to the surface again. Would she leave if there was nothing else to talk about?

"Will you please send me your schedule for the coming week, ma'am?" he asked.

She looked away before turning her eyes on him. "No. I mean, I don't have a schedule. Or plans. I don't have any plans for the week." She cleared her throat. "I think it's best to stay in for the next little while."

The media. "How long do you think that will be, ma'am?"

"At least a week. That's all I can tell you for now."

He nodded. "I understand." He couldn't blame her for not wanting that kind of attention.

"Maybe you can take some time off, Mr. Sterling," she said.

"Thank you for the suggestion, ma'am. If you change your mind, or need anything, anything at all, will you let me know?"

"Thank you, I will. Have a good day, Mr. Sterling."

"Good day, Your Highness."

He watched her leave and wanted to call her back, wanted to make her promise that she would contact him for any reason, that she wouldn't avoid him until the next official business. Because, somehow, if felt like she would evade him.

Why did she suggest the time off? Was she mad at him for kissing her? She hadn't been at the time, but maybe now, after thinking about it, after being away from him, she couldn't stand the kiss, couldn't stand him. Maybe that was the reason why she didn't even want him in the palace.

He passed the next two hours writing a detailed report of the time that he and Emma had been missing, explaining his decision for not notifying the others of their side trip while still keeping her privacy. Her secrets were hers to tell, and he had to take responsibility for his poor professional judgment and accept the consequences.

Chief Officer Peters approached Ryan in the computer room. "Sterling, I received a memo from Her Highness Princess Emma granting you paid time off."

"Yes, sir," Ryan replied. It looked like mandatory time off to him. Did she not want him around, or did she remember him saying he was due for a visit with Nana? Either way, he wasn't needed, and he was leaving. Would he be able to make things right again between him and Emma? Would he even have the chance?

"Take a couple of days," Peters added. "We'll see you back on Wednesday morning."

"Thank you, sir."

An hour later, Ryan was halfway to Nana Sterling's home. It hadn't taken long to pack and get ready for an overnight visit. He should have called her first, but it had slipped his mind, and he wouldn't pull out his phone while he drove. Surprise visit; she always liked those. How long had it been since her last call?

As he parked the car and walked to the door of the old white washed house, the memories rushed in, all those years ago when he'd arrived, an angry and unloved teenager, and met Nana for the first time. A lifetime ago.

He knocked three times before the door opened to reveal an older Black teenager with a phone in one hand and a pair of earbuds around his neck.

"Yes?"

"Is Nana home?" Ryan asked.

"Nana, it's for you," the teen yelled over his shoulder, already walking away.

A few minutes later, Ryan heard her voice coming from down the hallway. "Who is it, Cooper?"

"I don't know. Some guy."

"And you left the door open for a stranger?" Nana asked.

"He asked for you by name. I figured he must be okay."

"Let's hope so." She pulled to the door and her eyes widened. "Ryan," she exclaimed, a smile on her lips.

"I know it's been a while, but I'm not a stranger." He smiled and stepped inside as she threw her arms at him.

Was it just his impression or did she have more wrinkles around her eyes, more silver hair than brown? Her frame felt more fragile as he returned the hug.

"Come in, come in. Why didn't you call to say you were coming? I'd have cooked your favorite."

"I didn't know I was coming until this morning."

She ushered him in to the living room. "Cooper, this is Ryan. He spent some time with me when he was about your age."

That was an understatement. Nana had saved him from a life of misery and petty crime.

"Hey." Cooper nodded. "I finished my chores and homework. Can I go meet my friends now?"

"Yes, just be back by dinnertime," Nana replied.

After Cooper left, Nana walked to the kitchen, and Ryan followed her.

"I didn't know you were still fostering." He leaned against the doorjamb.

She nodded. "Not as much as before, but I'll keep doing it for as long as I'm able and they'll let me."

"You're a treasure, Nana," he said, hoping his tone lent the gratitude and admiration he wanted his words to convey.

She walked to the refrigerator and opened the door. "Did you have lunch yet? I made minestrone yesterday."

Ryan took a chair at the kitchen table. "Then I'll take some. I know better than to pass on your minestrone."

Within minutes, she had a large bowl of warmed soup and a generous slice of toasted bread on the table.

She took the chair next to him. "So, what brought about your visit this time? Not that I'm complaining. I love to have you back, for as long as you can stay."

"Until tomorrow, if that's okay." He'd leave after lunch, maybe early afternoon, which should give him plenty of time to tend to any small repairs around the house and yard, or anything else she might need.

"Of course. There's plenty of room upstairs. I'll help you make the bed later."

"If you keep the linens in the same closet, I can make it myself. And thank you."

"Don't even mention it, Ryan. You know you're always welcome."

He did know that. If he'd ever had a home, this was it, with Nana Sterling. "It was time. It's been a long while." He took his plate, bowl, and utensils to the sink and quickly washed them, then set them on the drying rack.

"And you needed a break," Nana said.

He nodded. "Just a short one. I don't have to be back until Wednesday morning."

"Those pictures I saw of Princess Emma in the news during her trip up north. Was that you with her?" Typical Nana—always direct.

Ryan nodded. "Yeah, that was me."

"I know better than to believe everything the media says . . ." The implied question hung in the air.

"But some parts are true," he admitted. "I drove the princess to see a property, and on the way back, we got stranded without cell coverage. We stayed with this couple for a few days, with no phone and no electricity. That's the gist of it," he added.

"It's only natural if you two got close during that time."

"We did, but it's complicated."

"Of course it is. Nothing worthwhile is ever simple."

Ryan took a deep breath. "I don't know what's worthwhile anymore."

"You do, Ryan. I know you do, and you know it as well."

Did he? Was he ready to pursue an uncertain future at the expense of the goals he'd worked so hard to achieve?

"Do I have to remind you of all the conversations we had at this very table? You always had the drive to succeed, of course, but your desire for a family of your own and people in your life to care about and who care about you was also there. Career and family are not mutually exclusive. Don't forget that."

Ryan spent the afternoon going through the house and yard and fixing whatever he could find—a leaky faucet in the upstairs bathroom, a stuck lock in the back door—then changed the oil in Nana's old car and took it for a wash and topped off the gas tank. He kept her words in the back of his mind, turning them over, trying to find a way to make everything work.

On Tuesday, after poking around Nana's pantry and freezer, and not finding much, he went to the local market and shopped for staples, canned goods, and frozen meats and vegetables.

Cooper arrived from school, and Ryan called him to the kitchen.

"What's going on?" The teen stopped at the door and looked around.

"I stocked up." Ryan emptied another bag. "Come help me put everything away, and then we can make dinner."

"It's kind of early for dinner."

"I have to leave tonight so I can be at work early tomorrow morning." Ryan filled the bottom drawer in the refrigerator with vegetables.

"Where's Nana?" Cooper asked.

"She went to see a neighbor and will be back soon."

"Is this your idea of male bonding?"

"No, this is my idea of getting you to help me so the work goes faster."

Cooper chuckled. "At least you're honest, and that's something I can appreciate." He pulled his sleeves back and walked to the sink to wash his hands. "What's for dinner?"

"Meatballs with spaghetti and sauce, salad, and garlic bread." Ryan gathered the ingredients. "Do you want to brown the meatballs or chop the onion?"

"I'll take the meatballs."

They worked at opposite sides, Cooper at the stove while Ryan chopped vegetables.

"So do you really work as the bodyguard to the princess?" Cooper asked after a few minutes.

Ryan lifted a questioning eyebrow, and Cooper continued. "I heard you and Nana talking."

Ryan nodded. "Yes, I'm Princess Emma's personal protection officer."

"What's it like? Do you follow her everywhere?"

"There's more to being a protection officer than following Her Highness. Being a part of Royal Security is an honor and a big responsibility." Ryan added a can of chopped tomatoes to the onions in the pot.

"But if she goes on a date, you go too, right?"

Ryan's mind jolted at the idea, and he barely kept himself from reacting physically. "Yeah, I'll go with Princess Emma when she dates." How would he deal with seeing Emma date another man? "Every time she leaves the palace, I accompany her."

Cooper asked more questions about Ryan's job, and it was all Ryan could do to keep his side of the conversation going while they finished cooking, his mind turning with too many unwanted scenarios of Emma going on dates. Despite what he'd just told Cooper, he wouldn't want to follow her around and witness her falling in love with another man. That would be too much, too painful to watch.

But wouldn't it happen that way if he did nothing about it?

When Nana returned, she supervised Cooper while he made the salad. Ryan removed the garlic bread from the oven, and they sat down to eat. Although none of them were related by blood, it felt like a family meal, somehow.

After they ate and cleared the dishes, Nana pulled out an old photo album.

"This is my family scrapbook." She set it down on the table. "All the children that have come through here, that made this house a home, and made me a mother. Even though I didn't give birth to any of them."

Ryan had heard it before. First, she hadn't been able to conceive, and then her husband had died too young. Instead of accepting her circumstances, she'd gone after what she wanted anyway.

She thumbed through the pages as he and Cooper looked on, and she remembered each child, their name, their story. Of course, Cooper took a special interest in Ryan's.

Nana was right. He'd lost sight of his goals, of his dreams, as focused as he'd been on his career and financial gain. The years were slipping by, and he wasn't doing anything toward his desire—no, his need—for a family of his own. If he continued on this path, he'd lose what mattered most, even before he obtained it—a relationship with Emma.

Was he ready to sacrifice his job? He wouldn't be able to continue as her protection officer, it would be a conflict of interest, but maybe he'd have the chance to ask to be reassigned.

Could he even date Emma if he wanted? *If* she wanted him, was the bigger question. Was there a protocol she had to follow for dating? From what he knew, her brother and cousins had married of their own free will, but he should find out for sure.

Ryan ended up leaving a bit later than he'd planned, but the time with Nana had been worth it, and he promised to visit more often, a promise he intended to keep. He lived closer now, even if he transferred somewhere else.

Now he just needed the courage to make changes and pursue his dream.

Chapter Twenty-Three

*E*mma had been avoiding her social duties and outings, and Ryan by extension, since they'd returned from what she had come to consider a life-changing trip. Wasn't it a type of cowardliness, this inability to face truth and reality? She'd even granted him paid time-off, and he'd gone away; Mr. Peters had confirmed it.

In the little moments she let her guard down long enough, her mind and heart filled with memories of Ryan, of all the time they'd spent together, and she missed him so much more than she ever thought possible. For someone who had only recently entered her life, he'd become one of the most important people in it.

At least one good thing had resulted from the trip—she finally had decided what to take on as her public charity cause.

She knocked on Aunt Nicolette's office door, and Mr. Poe opened it for her.

"Emma, dear, there you are. Right on schedule." Aunt Nicolette stood to meet her.

They exchanged air kisses. "Thanks for making time for me, Aunt Nicolette. I know how busy you are."

"I'll always make time for you, Emma." They sat down on the facing sofas. "Besides, I've been curious all morning to find out the reason for your visit. When Mr. Poe told me I had a work appointment with you, I could hardly wait."

Emma smiled. "You've been so patient with me, Aunt, and I wanted you to be the first to know."

"The first, you say? You haven't talked to Charlotte about it?"

"Not yet, I haven't."

"Is it about your charity cause, then?"

"Yes, Aunt. I've made a decision." She let out an internal sigh, relieved Aunt Nicolette didn't ask about her time away, then pulled out the tablet. "Did you know there are currently over twenty thousand children in Durham who will age out of the foster system before they're adopted? And when they turn eighteen, twenty percent of them will instantly become homeless?"

Aunt Nicolette took the tablet from her. "How did you come about these numbers and statistics?"

"I researched them myself, mainly with access to the Ministry of Education website."

"Is this what you've been doing all week? You've hardly come out from your apartment since you returned." Aunt Nicolette continued to scroll through the pages on the screen.

Emma nodded. "Choosing this cause was the easy part, but I wanted to be prepared, not only to present to you, but also for myself."

"This shows great maturity and thinking, Emma. I'm impressed. Congratulations on making a decision and doing such thorough research. Please send Mr. Poe a copy so he can print it for me." She handed the tablet back to Emma. "After struggling for so long with a choice, I can't help but wonder how you came to this decision." Aunt Nicolette tipped her head.

Emma hesitated for a moment. "I learned of someone's story who grew up in the foster system and didn't have good experiences. Fortunately, a kind woman came into his life when he was an older teenager. He was able to outgrow his difficulties, and his story turned out all right in the end—but that's not the case for the great majority of children who don't get adopted when they're younger."

"How do you see your involvement in this?" Aunt asked.

"I'd like to use part of my trust fund to jumpstart the charity and sponsor the first home for kids who have aged out of the system. As much as protocol would let me, my goal is to oversee what I can, keeping in mind that the privacy and safety of the children is paramount."

Emma no longer wanted to pursue the purchase of the property at Hillside Meadows; it was too far from Castlebridge and it needed too much work. Instead, she wished to transfer her efforts toward the new plan.

Aunt Nicolette nodded. "Go on."

"Fundraising would also have a big part, as long as it's not impersonal, and goes beyond charity balls or dinners. No offense," she added quickly.

"None taken," Aunt Nicolette said.

"I'd also like to form a special task force that can work more effectively at the local level for community outreach and offer opportunities for involvement."

"You've thought of everything, haven't you?"

"I'm sure I haven't, and I know there will be problems along the way, but I think I have what I need to get started. With your permission, of course," Emma added.

"You have it, Emma."

"I was also hoping you could mentor me, Aunt," Emma suggested.

"Yes, absolutely." Aunt Nicolette tapped her chin. "In fact, I have the perfect project coming up. There's a fundraising ball under my patronage to benefit the Durham Cancer Society."

"Isn't that next week?"

Aunt nodded. "I can bring you aboard the planning meetings to shadow me as I oversee the last details. It'll be busy, but you'll gain experience."

"Thank you, Aunt Nicolette. That will be amazing."

"I'll have Mr. Poe send you my calendar, and we can start on Monday."

They discussed a schedule that would leave time for Emma to continue with her research while helping with the fundraising ball.

"We'll have to tell the rest of the family as soon as possible. They'll be so excited. And please let me know what you need as you dive into it." They stood, and Aunt Nicolette briefly hugged Emma. "Your parents would be immensely proud of you. I hope you know that."

Emma nodded, unable to find the words, her throat clogged with emotion.

"And, Emma?" Aunt called. "I'm glad you found a cause, but don't forget your personal life. Don't hide. Take some chances." She winked at Emma.

Did her aunt know about her and Ryan? It wouldn't surprise her if she did.

As Emma walked back to her apartment, Aunt Nicolette's words stuck with her. Did she want to take some chances in her personal life? Was she ready to put her heart on the line? What if Ryan wasn't?

Once back at her desk, Emma worked on a priority list and calendar of tasks organized by day and week. Since it was Friday, she would start the process of choosing people to work with her next week.

When her phone rang with a video call from Charlotte, Emma grabbed it and hit accept.

"Where have you been all day? I tried to call you earlier," Charlotte said.

Emma sat down on the sofa and pulled her legs up on the ottoman directly in front. "I have so much to tell you, Char."

"Good things, I hope."

"Really good things." Emma grinned before continuing. "I've found my purpose in life, and I've never been busier."

"What happened? Last time we talked, you seemed so depressed. Did you and Ryan make up?"

Emma pressed her eyes closed for a second, then shook her head. "I haven't seen him since Monday, the day after we returned. I gave him paid time off and he went away for a couple of days. When he returned, I texted him and told him I didn't have any plans for the rest of the week nor the weekend, and that was it."

"That was it?" Charlotte repeated. "How much longer are you going to avoid him?"

"I really do have a lot going on. I'm not making that up."

"I believe you, Emma, but I also know you could easily make time for him, if you wanted to. I went through all that with Adam, keeping myself as busy as I could so I wouldn't have to see him. Take my word, it's just a miserable way of dealing with it."

"I remember," Emma said softly. "How is it possible, Char, that I feel so connected to him? I can't make sense of it. I've tried, and I can't."

"It is possible, and it doesn't have to make sense. Some connections are magical like that and go beyond reason. Just don't lose the connection because you're afraid."

Was it fear that held Emma back? "I can't see how it could work between me and Ryan. How can I ask him to quit his job? It's his career. He's worked so hard at it."

"You can't assume what he wants until you talk to him. It's not fair to him, or you. And might I remind you, you're not the only one who had to face obstacles in a relationship. Alex and Stefan have American wives, and Henry and Oliver married commoners. Even Adam and I had to make sacrifices."

Emma sighed. "I don't know what to do."

"I'm sorry, that sounded preachier than I intended. I just want to save you from making the same mistakes

I did." Charlotte changed the subject. "Tell me about this great news. What is it?"

Emma took a big breath and released it slowly. "I've finally made a decision about a cause to sponsor."

Charlotte's eyes widened, and she smiled. "You need to tell me everything," she exclaimed.

Emma related her meeting with Aunt Nicolette, told Charlotte all the details, and answered all the questions about her plans for the charity. For the next few minutes, they brainstormed names and ideas for raising funds, and Emma was looking forward to Charlotte's arrival in December so they could meet in person.

Later, Charlotte's words about Ryan tarried in Emma's mind. Was it fear or something more? Was she ready to offer her heart with no expectations?

Chapter Twenty-Four

Ryan held the car door open for Emma, and she slipped inside with a quiet thanks. He signaled the driver, and they pulled out toward the city center.

After a week spent at the palace without going anywhere, she'd started this week in a whirlwind of outings. Every day she'd gone somewhere, either in the morning or in the afternoon, sometimes both—running errands, attending meetings, visiting different locations. Of course, wherever she went, he did too, and so did one of the drivers, which meant they didn't have any moments alone.

But despite the physical proximity, they stood farther away from each other than they had in the beginning. How was he supposed to go on as her protection officer? Seeing her and not touching her?

Watching her life go by and standing at the fringe, never being a part of it?

He had his limits.

When they arrived at the Plaza Hotel in downtown Castlebridge, Ryan accompanied Emma to the grand salon where the fundraising ball was scheduled to take place this Saturday evening. She met with the event coordinator, and the two of them went through the program with the master of ceremonies, the menu with the chef, the lighting with the main technician, and the music with the pianist. Chief Officer Peters was in charge of coordinating with hotel security. After, Emma and the coordinator checked all the tables, centerpieces, place cards, and seating arrangements. No detail was too small, too unimportant, and he'd never seen her so focused before.

Through it all, he remained to the side, observing the protocol distance, not too far and not too close; just enough to watch her and intervene, if necessary.

Three hours later, Emma nodded at the hotel coordinator, who gave a short curtsy, signaling the end of their meeting. Ryan squared his shoulders and met her halfway, then guided her to the VIP elevator.

Once the doors closed, she rested against the wall and kneaded the back of her neck.

"Tired?" he asked. He shouldn't have asked something personal, but he craved the connection with her.

"Just some tension." She gave him a small, weary smile.

Would she let him massage her neck? He spied the cameras at the opposite corners on the ceiling of the elevator cab, and his crazy thought fizzled immediately. Instead he straightened and added some distance between them, his hands to his sides.

"You've been working really hard for this event."

"Aunt Nicolette put her trust in me, and I don't want to disappoint her. Besides, it's good training."

She was in training? For what? How had he missed that? It all made sense, given her many meetings with Her Majesty and her demanding schedule.

At the royal suite, he opened the door, and they stepped inside. "Wait here, please." He made the necessary safety checks and returned to her. "All clear."

"Thank you, Ryan." She crossed to the nearest sofa and sat down.

Did his name slip, or was it intentional? She hadn't used his first name since their time at the Baxters'. He missed the way she said it.

"I'll text you when I'm ready to go down to the grand salon," she said.

It was a dismissal, but Ryan didn't move. "What's your schedule like for the afternoon?"

She looked at the clock on the mantel. "The stylist and hairdresser should be here in about one hour to help me get ready."

"Let's call up a meal, then." He pulled out his phone for the room service app.

"Nothing too heavy. I'm a ball of nerves already, and don't want a belly ache."

"Vegetable soup and toast?" he suggested.

"That will be perfect, thank you." Another pale smile.

He nodded and finished placing the order. "It'll be here in ten minutes. Do you have the time to rest?"

She shook her head. "If I rest, I'll fall asleep, which will make me late and more stressed."

"We don't want that. You have enough stress already." He pulled out the app again, this time for services. "What about a chair massage? Twenty minutes to help you relax and ease your tension before the event."

Her expression bloomed. "A chair massage? That seems so decadent. I don't think I should."

"It's my job to look after you, and I say you totally should." Before she refused, he booked it. "All done. The massage therapist will be here in thirty minutes. You'll be finished well before the hairdresser and stylist arrive." He returned the phone to his pocket, a self-satisfied smile tugging at the corner of his mouth—she wouldn't have booked the massage herself, so he'd done it for her.

She sat up and her eyes went wide. "Ryan, you didn't."

He stood his ground. "Yes, I did, Emma." He paused and added, "Ma'am."

She regarded him softly. "You don't have to ma'am me when it's the two of us."

Only he did. If he didn't, he wouldn't be able to stay away from her, and that would ruin his plan. There was no other way; he had to stick to the plan.

Her blue eyes almost undid him, and he nodded at her half-heartedly, not wanting to contradict her and be forced to give explanations he wasn't ready to offer.

A knock sounded at the door, and relief rushed through him at the interruption. "That will be your lunch."

He let the server push in the rolling tray and set the lunch on the table, then tipped the young woman and let her out.

Emma lifted the domed cover. "It smells so good. I'm actually hungrier than I thought." She took a seat and gestured to the chair closest to her. "Will you join me? There's enough for two."

"I'll wait until the masseuse comes." He picked an apple from the fruit bowl and sat down at a different chair.

She eyed his choice. "Since when is an apple enough lunch?"

"I'll order something else before my tux comes."

She looked up from her soup and raised an eyebrow. "You're wearing a tuxedo tonight?"

"Chief Officer Peters was adamant," he replied. "All Royal Security and protection officers need to wear full black tie." Ryan didn't like the formality, but he didn't have a choice.

An interested gleam filled her features, and she tipped her head to the side. "Lumberjack to black tie. You're versatile."

"May I ask you a question?"

"Of course," she replied in between spoonfuls of soup.

"You said this event is good training. What's the training for?" He placed the apple core on a small plate.

"Aunt Nicolette is mentoring me on how to plan and run fundraising events."

"Is this a new interest, or has it always been the plan?"

She opened her mouth to reply, but a knock at the door interrupted her.

Ryan opened the door to find the massage therapist. He inspected her credentials and equipment, then indicated for her to set up. "I'll be in my room next door, ma'am. Please text me if you need anything."

"I'll be all right. Thank you, Ryan." Her eyes swept over the lunch and the massage chair.

"You're welcome, ma'am. At what time would you like to go down?"

"The event starts at eight, but I'd like to be there an hour earlier for a final check."

"Very well. I'll return at seven to escort you to the salon." He bowed from the neck and exited.

Once in his bedroom, Ryan removed his tie and suit coat and kicked off his shoes. He had over four hours to kill, but it was too early to shave and get in the shower.

Knowing Emma was in the room next door, with only a wall separating them, filled his head with all kinds of thoughts he shouldn't entertain. He rubbed the back of his neck and walked to the windows.

They'd talked less formally today, less awkwardly, almost like they had at the Baxters'. But it wouldn't last. That much he knew. How could it, really?

Ryan knocked on the door across from his at seven on the dot. He'd showered, shaved, and changed into the tuxedo, shoulder holster in place.

A soft "Coming" sounded from within and he waited, the awareness washing over him that something would happen tonight. But what? The gut feeling persisted.

The door opened wide, and his jaw dropped—Emma was a vision and he had no words.

"Wow," she said, taking him in from top to bottom. "So sharp. You should wear a tux more often."

He barely registered her compliment, unable to look away from her.

She stood in a strapless gown, fitted through the bodice and hips, flaring widely above the knees, a fantasy of shimmering blue with purple undertones, like a mermaid emerging from the foamy spray. Her hair was done in a low bun, intricately woven and clasped with a vintage-looking comb, most likely a family heirloom. He'd seen pictures of her in evening gowns, but this one looked amazing on her.

He couldn't stop staring, still awestruck and wordless.

Emma's cheeks tinted under his perusal, and the blush added more to her beauty.

He finally recovered his wits. "Your Highness." He bowed to her, even though they were alone. "You look magnificent." It was the truth, but the words felt trite. If only he could show her everything he couldn't say.

Her eyebrows knitted. "I wish you'd stop that."

He didn't have to ask what—the title and the bow, of course. To him, it was a reminder to keep his emotional distance even more than the physical. His heart yearned for her even as his mind told him to stay away.

The rest of the evening stretched in bittersweet agony for him. Emma was truly magnificent, and not only for how she looked in that exquisite dress. The way she oversaw the event, in complete control through the silent auction, the dinner, her aunt's appearance and brief speech, and lastly, the dance.

He was never too far from her, maybe closer than he should have been, given the event was so heavily guarded. All night he listened and watched those who approached her, wishing in vain for what he couldn't have—her attention, a seat beside her at dinner, her arms in his on the dance floor.

If nothing else, it all attested to the list of reasons he kept in the back of his mind, why he couldn't continue like this.

Emma thanked the guy she'd danced with and excused herself with a smile. The event was winding down, and she had to be tired. She glanced Ryan's way, and he followed right behind, but instead of taking the path to the service elevator, she veered to a short hallway and took a sharp left.

Where was she going?

"Your Highness?" he called from the open doorway. The light inside the room was off, and he couldn't see her.

"In here," came her voice, much closer than he'd believed her to be.

He felt along the wall for the light switch.

Her hand clamped on his. "Leave it." The words fanned his neck, and his skin prickled.

"What's going on?"

"I want to dance with you, Ryan, and I can't do that in front of a grand salon full of people watching my every move."

She was right. "We shouldn't," he said to her.

After his eyes adjusted to the dim light, he found her standing in front of him. Emma raised her arms into position, and he did the same, welcoming her into his embrace. The faint strains of a waltz played in the background, just enough music to carry them around the floor.

Somehow, they gravitated closer together, the low ruffles of her dress tangling in between his pant legs. He couldn't tell who'd eclipsed the distance first, him or her—did it even matter? They had been in each other's orbit until a collision was only inevitable.

Her scent and her warmth wafted to him, and Ryan closed his eyes.

Bittersweet torture.

A yearning concession.

The beginning or the end?

She broke the silence first. "Tell me, is this how it's going to be with us now, as if we don't know each other? Principal and protection officer, and nothing more?"

"No." His voice came out like gravel, and he cleared his throat. "No, it isn't." He hadn't planned to tell her like this. "This is my last night on the job. I handed in my resignation this morning."

Her arms dropped from his, and she froze. "You what?"

He swallowed.

For a long moment, they regarded each other, standing in the shaft of spilled light from the hallway.

"You're not serious," Emma said, her voice low. "You can't be."

He took a step back. "I can't stay. I can't stay as your protection officer," he repeated in a firmer tone.

"Why not? I need a protection officer, now more than ever."

"It doesn't have to be me," he reasoned. "They can assign any of the other officers for your protection detail, and they'll do a great job. Maybe even better than I have."

Emma shook her head, then squared her shoulders and stepped up to him. "But I need you. You can't leave."

He held her gaze, willing her to understand. "Why do you need me, Emma? I'm not special. You can choose anyone else. Why *me*?"

She searched his eyes, and something slowly shifted in her expression. "You're right. I should ask for someone else to be my protection officer."

Ryan's heart twisted at her words. This is what he'd wanted, her agreement. He waited for the relief to follow, but it didn't come. Why did it hurt to know she finally agreed with him? It didn't matter; it would be easier this way.

He nodded slowly and glanced away. "Thank you. I'll take care of it when we get back to the palace."

"But you're wrong too," Emma added.

He lifted his head her way and frowned. "What am I wrong about?"

"You *are* special, Ryan Sterling."

Chapter Twenty-Five

*E*mma's hands shook. She clasped them in front of her and held firm. Inside, she trembled and teetered on the edge of her world, waiting.

The intensity of Ryan's gaze bore into hers, confusion filling his expression. Was that hope as well, or did she see what she wished to find there?

Did she have the courage to continue, to give this man her love, even if he didn't love her back?

Somehow, the clarity was stark to her—she had to tell him how she felt, whatever the outcome. He had to know.

"You are very special to me. I choose you." She swallowed and forged on. "I—I need you. I want you. You are my friend. And I think I'm falling in love with you." She cleared her throat. "Actually, I know I'm in love with you."

"Emma," he said in a whisper.

She waited, her heart beating faster and faster, the blood in her veins rushing louder and louder with every second. She had just bared her heart to him, but he remained silent and staring, almost stunned.

"That's all I wanted to say. I'm going back now." She turned to leave. Maybe she'd take the service elevator and escape to her suite instead; she couldn't face anyone right now.

"Wait, wait, wait," his words tumbled out in a single breath. He caught up to her and touched her shoulder. "You can't go without me. You can't say all that and just leave."

At the contact of his fingers on her bare skin, she whirled about. "Well, I am going, and I won't take my words back either."

His hands cradled her face, and he rested his forehead on hers. "Hush, hush. I'm a fool, Emma. I'm the fool who loves you so much, I can barely say the words, any words. Please, forgive me."

She sagged against him, weak-muscled and light-headed, hands locked behind his neck, relief spilling out and tears welling unchecked. His hands moved to her waist and he brought her flush against him. When she tipped her lips to him, he kissed her.

It was all at once familiar and different, just like Ryan was, like coming home to him. He didn't rush, his mouth lingering effortlessly. The touch of his lips ignited hers, the soft, sensitive skin like a fire between them, a long, languorous flaming she didn't want to stop.

"I had to quit, Emma." He touched a kiss to her lips again. "I couldn't think of another way to have a chance with you." He trailed little kisses on her face and jaw, returning to her mouth.

Somehow Ryan found a chair and sat on it, pulling her onto his lap, her dress falling over the side of his legs in billows and ruffles. Her arms closed more firmly around his frame, and their mouths found each other. Again and again.

"I looked up the dating protocol," he said, his words falling like a confession.

Her fingertips brushed the back of his neck, the small hairs there, the smooth skin turning to goose bumps. "There's no protocol."

"There's no protocol for dating," he repeated, kissing her longer, deeper, his scent and taste swirling her senses. "I can date you."

"I know. Please do." Between words and kisses, their breath mingled and teased, their faces touched. "I don't want you to be my protection officer." This was her confession.

"Good. I don't want to be your protection officer either. I'll be too busy taking care of your heart."

Emma sighed. "You're the one I love, the one I want," she whispered. "I love you."

Ryan caught her mouth in another kiss. "It's amazing that you feel the same way I do." He took her hand and splayed it over his chest. "My heart is yours. I love you."

She brought her hands to frame his face and they kissed again.

After a long minute, he pulled away, leaving a shaky breath in his wake. "We should go. Are you done in there?" He tipped his chin toward the salon.

"Completely done." She stood, her knees still wobbly, a languid warmth in her chest and a delicious numbness in her lips.

Ryan's arm came around her waist. "Let's get you back to your suite."

When they arrived at her door, he opened it for her, then leaned against the doorjamb, blocking her from view if anyone passed by. "I'm not ready to let you go," he whispered.

She wasn't either. "I need ten minutes to change. This corset is killing me."

"I didn't even tell you how amazing this dress looks on you." His gaze lingered on her. "I never had the chance."

"Thank you." She turned around. "Now give me a hand, please. There's a little hook just above the zipper."

He shuddered. "You're killing me, Emma."

Her skin pebbled when he touched her back. Her light chuckles didn't help his task, and he fumbled for another minute before succeeding.

"I'll go to my room now, and I'll meet you here in a few minutes. Is that okay?" Ryan asked.

She nodded. "That will be great."

By the time he returned, they had changed into comfortable clothes, and Emma had ordered latenight snacks from room service. They sat on the sofa next to each other, turned on the television for ambient noise, and lowered the lights. Soon, all of that was forgotten in the nearly darkened suite as the kisses continued in earnest for a little while until they trailed lazily, both of them too relaxed, too tired to think beyond the moment and the comfort of each other's company.

"What time is it?" she asked, groggily.

Ryan fetched his phone from his pocket and peeked at the screen. "Almost one in the morning."

"Are you going back to your room?"

"I'm staying until you tell me to go."

Contentment flashed through her and turned into a little smile. "Don't go."

"I won't."

"We have so much to talk about." Her voice came weak, as she fought the sleep that threatened to overtake her. She didn't want to miss any time with

Ryan, none, but the day had been long and much had happened, especially between them.

He nuzzled the side of her neck and kissed the spot behind her hear. "I know, but it can wait. You're half-asleep already, and I'll be there soon." He tightened his arms around her. "Let me hold you like this for a little while longer."

She settled against him and whispered near his ear. "Please hold me like this for always."

"I will, sweetheart. I will."

What more could they want but each other?

Epilogue

Early December

*E*mma rapped on the door, barely able to contain her excitement. Charlotte and Adam had arrived yesterday, later in the day than expected, due to some delays in their trip. Despite looking forward so much to her cousin's arrival, Emma had given them the time and privacy to rest last night. But it was morning now, and she couldn't wait any longer.

Charlotte opened the door, and they fell into each other's arms, with tight hugs and laughs, and even a few tears.

"I can't believe you're finally here." Emma stepped back and looked at her cousin. "You look so amazing, and your baby bump is adorable. How are you feeling?"

"A little tired, but I actually slept well."

"And the baby?"

"Kicking up a storm, as always."

"She needs to take it easy," Adam piped up.

"Yes, you do," Emma readily agreed. "I'll take good care of you, we all will."

Adam greeted Emma with a quick kiss on the cheek. "It's great to see you, Emma. That's all she talks about: Emma this, Emma that." He smiled and took Charlotte in his arms for a kiss. "I'm glad you two are finally reunited."

"I am too," Emma and Charlotte said at the same time, then laughed together.

"Do you have a few minutes before breakfast?" Emma asked.

"I already had breakfast, but don't tell Mother and Father," Charlotte said. "They asked Adam and I to join them for breakfast this morning, and I'll be ready to eat again by then. I'm always hungry lately. What do you need?"

"You haven't peeked in the nursery yet, have you?" Emma had finished decorating in November and could hardly wait to show it off to Charlotte. She'd tied a bow on the door handle with a sign saying *No peeking allowed*.

"I wanted to, but I was good. You know how I love surprises."

Adam joined them in front of the nursery, which was next to the master bedroom.

Emma held up her phone. "You two turn around. I'll film you from inside to record your reactions when you come in."

They did as she asked. Emma entered the room and closed the door behind her, then pressed the button to start the video recording. "Come on in. I'm ready."

Charlotte entered first, a wide smile on her face, and Adam right behind her.

"Whoa," he said.

Charlotte gasped. Her hands covered her mouth, and tears ran down her face as she looked around.

Emma's expression dropped. "Do you not like it? Should I stop filming?"

"Oh my goodness," Charlotte said at last. "This is amazing, Emma. It's so beautiful." She went around the room, slowly taking everything in—the bookcase with all the books, the crib and wardrobe, the mural, the play area, the rocking chair and rug, all the little touches that held the meaning and history of Charlotte and Adam's relationship.

Emma smiled. "You had me worried for a minute with those tears."

"Happy tears, Em, happy tears. Come here and give me a hug."

Emma turned off her phone and slipped it into her pocket, then stepped into her cousin's arms.

"How can I ever thank you?" Charlotte asked. "I could have never imagined such a beautiful nursery."

She rested a hand on her growing belly. "This little one is so spoiled already."

"So loved," Emma corrected. "And no thanks needed. It was my absolute pleasure."

"Look at me, you two, and squish closer," Adam said, then held up his phone to take a photo of them.

After a few minutes explaining some of the objects, they walked back to the living room.

"I'd better go and leave you to your second breakfast," Emma teased.

Adam chuckled. "See, I'm not the only one to call it that."

Charlotte shook her head good naturedly, then turned to Emma. "When do I get to meet Ryan?"

"Are you free this evening? We should meet for dinner."

"Yes, let's do that. And good luck this afternoon," Charlotte added.

Emma smiled. "Thanks. I'm going to need a big dose of it." She had the official press release to announce the launching of the Coming Home project and the groundbreaking for the first group home for at-risk teens in Castlebridge. "I don't know if I'm more nervous or more excited about it. It's all a jumble inside."

"You'll do great. I'll make sure to watch it on the news. And I can't wait to meet Ryan."

They exchanged goodbyes and hugs.

Emma slipped into her apartment to retrieve her purse and laptop bag, then called Ryan.

"Hey, sweetheart, did you see your cousin yet?"

She still melted every time he used the endearment. "I did, and she loves the nursery," Emma replied. "Such a relief."

"Of course she does. You did an amazing job with the design and decoration."

A light smile pulled on the corner of her lips. "I think your opinion might be a little biased, but I'll take it anyway."

"If thinking my girlfriend is amazing makes me biased, then I guess I am, and proudly so."

Her little smile grew into a silly grin. "When is your meeting?"

"In about ten minutes. I should probably go. I'll meet you before the press conference starts, and I'm all yours for the rest of the day."

"I really like the sound of that."

"I do too. I'll text you when I leave. I love you."

"I love you, too."

Emma's grin stayed on her face for a while longer, her heart filled with more love and contentment than she'd dreamed possible before meeting Ryan.

It was almost two and a half months since the fundraising ball when Emma and Ryan had confessed their feelings to each other. They had gone to Aunt Nicolette and Uncle Geoffrey the next day, who had advised them to not keep it private. By Monday, Ryan's resignation was official, and Mr. Little had become Emma's new personal protection officer, giving Emma and Ryan the freedom to have a relationship.

The media was relentless that first week, clamoring for statements and photos ops, but Emma and Ryan had kept to themselves until the attention shifted to something more sensational, as it usually did.

To accommodate Emma's high-profile schedule and the demands of her new social project, Ryan had turned to freelance security consulting, and he made it a priority to accompany Emma on her public appearances to show his support and commitment.

After last-minute meetings and preparations that took the rest of the morning, Emma returned to her apartment in the royal wing to wait for Ryan.

A knock sounded at the door, and she opened it to find him there.

"You're early." She smiled, unable to stop herself every time she saw him. "I wasn't expecting you for another twenty minutes."

He stepped inside and locked an arm around her, then closed the door with his free hand. "The meeting went well and I got everything wrapped up quickly. I couldn't wait to see you." His smile matched hers, and his eyes twinkled.

Before she had a chance to say anything in return, he pulled her closer for a searing kiss, and they lost themselves in each other for a long moment.

"I missed you too," she said, when they came up for air.

She hadn't seen him since yesterday, and he looked good in his dark navy suit and pinstriped tie. Since leaving the Royal Security team, he kept a trimmed three-day beard that she found much too attractive. But more than his good looks, she liked him for the man he was, for his personality, intelligence, and kindness, and for how much better she was with him. They supported one another and made each other happy, and that was priceless.

She raised her fingers and caressed the side of his face, then reached to brush a kiss there. "Thank you for coming with me."

"Where else would I be, Emma, if not by your side?"

This man. How she loved him.

Warmth suffused her chest, and a sense of utter calm washed through her.

Life was good. So good indeed.

Two weeks later
The Somerset family Christmas party

Ryan looked around and smiled. For an intimate party, as Queen Nicolette had described it, there was a lot of family in attendance. All of them, in fact. In addition to her aunt and uncle, Emma's four cousins—Alex, Stefan, Henry, and Charlotte—and her brother, Oliver, and all their spouses and children, had made it together in one room, which hadn't happened in a while, according to Emma.

The room was large and heavily decorated for Christmas in traditional tones of red, green, and gold, with a laid-back atmosphere that reflected itself in how at ease everyone interacted with each other. Quite different from formal events, which suited him just fine.

These were Emma's people. She loved them, and they loved her, and he was glad for the chance to meet those he hadn't yet. With everyone's busy schedules and responsibilities, they had made an effort to spend time together for Christmas, and, despite the craziness and noise, there was a lot of love also. He could almost imagine how it must have been when they were younger, maybe even louder and crazier than it was now. For him, who'd grown up without family, there was a sense of magic.

It still amazed him how completely Emma accepted him for who he was, how she'd never balked at his lack of family history; she, who belonged to a pedigree that could trace their lineage for multiple generations. He'd had to learn to push his worries aside that he wasn't good enough to date a princess. The doubts were his, not anyone else's, and even her aunt and uncle had been firm in their support of Emma and Ryan's relationship. There were no impediments, no one opposed.

From his corner, his gaze followed Emma as she made her way around the room. He loved watching how her eyes shone, the way she laughed, and how happy she was tonight. Life wasn't about laughs and parties every day, but having a close family for support made all the difference when pain and sorrows came, as they were bound to come. Love made all the difference.

This was exactly what he wanted for himself and Emma—a crazy family of their own, passionate and happy, and even silly sometimes. There was nothing more important than this—certainly not his career— and there was no reason to wait any longer. He knew he couldn't go through the rest of his life without her and was sure she felt the same way about him. Waiting made no sense at all.

He was going to ask her tonight. Right now, actually. He'd been carrying the ring in his pocket for a few days, waiting for the perfect moment to ask her, and this was it. No more waiting.

As if she could hear his thoughts, Emma raised her eyes to him from across the room and winked with a little flirty smile. He chuckled and returned the wink, then tipped his head toward the hallway. She excused herself from the conversation and met him out in the corridor.

He pressed his mouth to hers in a chaste kiss, mindful of the people in the next room, who could interrupt at any time.

"You were watching me so intently," she said. "What's on your mind? Is all this a bit much?"

"No, it's just right, and I love it. Your family is awesome. All of them."

"They think you're awesome too."

He grinned. "That's good, then, since I have no plans to let go of you."

Her eyes crinkled at the corners as she smiled at him, and she reached up for a quick kiss. "Those are the best plans."

"How do you feel about going somewhere more private so I can kiss you properly?"

Her smile turned mischievous. "How can I say no to that?"

She took him by the hand and led him the opposite direction, into a small parlor, also decorated for Christmas.

Once they closed the door, Ryan pulled Emma into his arms and molded his mouth to hers, slowly taking his time, pouring all his feelings into a memorable kiss, into a moment he didn't want to forget.

She sagged against his chest and sighed. "Whoa. What a kiss. I think I need a few minutes before going back in there."

Ryan took her hands in his.

"You are so beautiful and I love you so much. I can't imagine loving you any more than I do now, but I want to try, if you'll have me."

She squeezed his hands. "Of course I'll have you. I thought I already did."

"Let's make it official, then." He slipped a hand in his pocket and removed the ring, then went down on one knee in front of her. "Emma, will you marry me?"

She gasped, and her hands flew to cover her mouth, a tear rolling down her cheek. "Oh my goodness. My goodness," she repeated, still rooted in place.

When she didn't say anything else, Ryan asked, "Is that a yes or a not yet?"

"Of course it's a yes, of course." She pulled at him to stand, and he slid the ring onto her left ring finger, both their hands shaking a bit.

"I don't have a ring that's been passed down in the family, but I thought we could start with our own."

"I love that idea, Ryan. The ring is beautiful, and I love you. Of course I'll marry you. How could you think I wouldn't?"

"I didn't want to presume."

She laughed and cried at the same time, then flung her arms around his neck and reached up to kiss him, but she kept smiling wide, and soon he was smiling as well.

"I know we haven't been together for too long, but it feels right."

She nodded. "It feels so right."

This time the kiss turned serious. After a minute, he said, "If we stay here, I'll be kissing you all night. Let's go tell your family before they come looking for us."

She laughed again. "I bet Oliver would. He likes to play the protective older brother."

"Yes, he was very serious in his advice when I told him I was going to ask you."

She stopped to look at him. "You did?"

"I also asked His Majesty for his blessing, and that was intimidating." Intimidating was an understatement.

"Uncle Geoffrey is a big teddy bear."

"Maybe to you, but he's not my uncle."

She chuckled. "He will be. And everyone else will be your family too."

"The more the merrier." He meant it too.

The walk back took longer, as they stopped several times to kiss before they arrived.

"Attention, everyone," he said at the door, his voice carrying above the din.

The noise quieted, and everyone turned to them, many of them questioning the interruption. Charlotte raised an eyebrow and mouthed something at Emma, who only smiled in reply.

After a pause for effect, he raised their joined hands and pumped them in the air. "She said yes."

The room erupted in hearty claps and congratulations.

"I knew it," Charlotte said, tightly hugging Emma. "The way he's been looking at you all night, I knew he was up to something."

So maybe someone had been paying attention.

Emma laughed. "I had no idea he was going to ask me." She lifted her left hand for Charlotte to inspect the ring, and the sisters-in-law flocked around them.

Oliver and the cousins rounded on Ryan with wishes of welcome and pats on the back, then turned to her with hugs and kisses. When King Geoffrey and Queen Nicolette approached, the rest of the family cleared room for them. They hugged Emma and shook Ryan's hand and congratulated them as well. Would he ever get used to having His and Her Majesties for in-laws?

As long as he had Emma—as long as they had each other—everything else was right.

She was his family, his home.

Dear Reader,

Thank you so much for reading Princess Emma and Ryan's story, *Protecting The Princess*. I hope you've enjoyed reading it as much as I enjoyed writing it.

Please consider leaving a review on Amazon and Goodreads. This is the best way to support me as an author.

For news of upcoming books and promotions, join my readers club.

I love to hear from readers! You can email me at lucinda@lucindawhitney.com.

Thank you!

Acknowledgments

The one thing nobody tells a new writer when they're working on their first book, is how the first book will not be the hardest one to write. Each book comes with a new set of challenges, and some of these are easier to solve than others, but they're always present. After all, writing is hard, even when the story is easy (which was not the case).

I started writing Protecting the Princess at a stressful time in my life. Then the pandemic hit and the quarantine was imposed, and that didn't help any. I had almost eighteen thousand words in the story when I realized none of them were working, so I scrapped them to start over. And then I couldn't write.

I spent the next few months, from the end of spring almost until the end of summer, painting walls and furniture, and completely redoing my kitchen. It was a lot of work, but well worth it.

Soon after, I started writing a new version, but got stuck, and had to ask my content editor for some suggestions (I have the best content editor, by the way). And slowly, very slowly, through the rest of winter, Emma and Ryan's story emerged.

At one point early on, I was convinced I'd never be able to finish it, so it's such a relief to see it published. I fell in love with Ryan and Emma along the way, after spending so much time in their company, and even learned to trust them when I ran out of hope.

Laura and Lindzee, thank you for all the brainstorming sessions, and general rants, and everything else, especially for always being as interested in Emma and Ryan as I am. It's eighteen months late, but it's finally here.

Thank you, Michele, for being the best content editor, for the suggestions and ideas, and always knowing just what the story needs.

Haley, thanks for taking this project on such short notice, and for your patience with my misuse of prepositions.

Thank you also to my review team and the great job they did in catching typos and small mistakes.

I'm also grateful for the encouraging words I've received from readers and friends that inspired me to keep going with this story.

About the Author

LUCINDA WHITNEY was born and raised in Portugal, where she received a Master's degree from the University of Minho in Braga, in Portuguese/English teaching.

She lives in northern Utah with her husband and four children. When she's not reading and writing, she can be found with a pair of knitting needles, or tending her herb garden.

She's the author of the Romano Family series, and the co-author of the Royal Secrets series with Lindzee Armstrong and Laura D. Bastian.

Please visit her website at lucindawhitney.com for more information and news.